# GO~~~~ ELEANOR

## A Heartbreaking Story

### BY
### NAS BEN

Copyright ©2024, Author Nas BEN

# GOODBYE ELEANOR

A Heartbreaking Story

By Nas Ben

# Dedication:

This book is for you, dear reader, and you alone. May you enjoy the story and live each moment within its pages."

## Author's note

As I placed the final full stop in this novel, I stood in astonishment at the culmination of its events.
It became evident to me that this narrative will likely invite significant critique and stirs countless inquiries. Therefore, I wish to clarify that these words do not represent the author's perspective, or that of any other entity, despite any resemblances in names, events, or locales.
There was no predetermined scheme for the unfolding events; instead, I allowed my pen to chart its course and reveal its own truths.
Ultimately, it is the voice of the pen that speaks here.

# Acknowledgement

It may seem strange, but it is the truth. I extend my heartfelt thanks to a song that appeared by chance on my social media screen, '11 AM Coffee.' Those moments were my muse and the gateway to this book.

**Author page:** Nas ben

Nas ben is a novelist and English teacher. His books include evocative storytelling and a unique perspective that have garnered attention in literary circles.

His debut novel, "Goodbye Eleanor" is expected to be a 5-star rated bestseller this year in Romance Literary Fiction, Women's Literary Fiction, and Contemporary Romance Fiction.

Driven by a passion for untold stories and a curiosity about women's experiences, Nas has cultivated his craft over time, experimenting across genres until finding his unique voice in artful romance storytelling.

" Goodbye Eleanor " stands as a testament to Nas's commitment to blending intriguing and controversial romance with narrative depth. Through intricate character dynamics and thematic exploration, the novel delves into loyalty, sacrifice, and the complexities of human relationships, offering readers a compelling literary experience.

Whether you're seeking a novelist with a flair for deep, engaging narratives or a writer with strong audacity, Nas ben brings a wealth of experience and creativity to every project.

Nas ben gives you joy, hope, and love through his writing.

# Chapter 1

Happy birthday... Whispering it alone to myself, sitting here with the door behind me, in that old London coffee shop at the end of the street reminiscing back and sipping my hot coffee like it's my lifeline, under the watchful gaze of the aged bay window painted in red. Countless are the times this black frame with branching cracks has listened to the sighs of lost souls who sat beside it. Even their sorrows etched wrinkles on her ribs.

I contemplate the coldest weather outside with thick clouds and foggy roads winding through the area, as if it's mirroring my inner thoughts, scattered and apprehensive. Tears fight my eyelids, trying not to fall onto my cheeks—untouched by another's hand for a long while.

I can't believe how quickly the years have flown by, like it has wings. These forty years carry secrets in every moment I've passed through and wisdom that blossoms after a long wait.

Forty years fluctuating between happy moments and tough challenges, hope and despair, love and revenge, hatred and longing.

Now, after all these flying years, which made me muddled, I stand bewildered, even fearful, of what other surprises tomorrow may hold. After all the deceit and deception I've experienced, I couldn't believe how a woman of my intelligence and depth find herself trapped in such a predicament? Is it the bragging of my blind self-confidence, or the folly whispered by those who claim wisdom in this age? Indeed, it is the forbidden love that I already knew beforehand to be impossible.

I spent an hour crying over my situation and reproaching my actions, until my anxieties faded away and the truth dawned on me. In the silent hush and tranquility, I reviewed all my past decisions one by one, carefully critiquing each one individually. Those self-help books, with their neatly packaged wisdom, were nothing but a comforting illusion, a mirage in the desert of my discontent. It feels like the ancient writers knew me better than these coaches who taught us swimming, then drowned, or those who offered us valuable psychological advice about the harms of drug addiction, then died from overdoses.

Before the last tear threatened to fall into my heart, the gentle door chime announced the arrival of a man wrapped in a brown muffler, wearing dark trousers, red shoes, and a coat with a black and gold pattern. I secretly looked up at this familiar silhouette, going straight to Eleanor.

He warmly greeted her "Eleanor, Good morning."

"Hey! James It's been too long," she replied, the hope in her voice genuine.

"Ah, you know...my children stole my time. I'm a prisoner," he answered with a laugh.

"Oh, I forgot, happy birthday to you, Eleanor," he adds, almost as< an afterthought.

"How did you know it's my birthday?" I Exclaimed, surprise etching my features. The familiarity of his knowledge, a reminder of a connection that time hadn't entirely erased.

"Facebook never lies," he acknowledged with a chuckle, the twinkle in his eye betraying a mix of jest and truth.

She forced a smile and said, "Thank you anyway, James."

"Your Americano, James!" calls the barista, her voice a bright note amidst the café's gentle buzz...

"Got to run," James said, flashing a quick smile. "Good to see you. Catch you later." He left and disappeared into the fog."

As the sturdy door gently closed before my eyes, a gaping chasm suddenly opened in my heart and mind.

"I no longer desire this brief encounter." I hooked decisively.

Years have taught me how to succeed in this individualistic society, where achievement is paved with the currency of personal sacrifice. But one thing eludes me still - the feeling of solitude... Until a hand grabbed me and took me out of the café..

Returning home, I observed the scene in the garden court as I made my way through Hyde Park. Despite the chilly weather, the warmth of solitude was thawing the freeze, as everyone was engrossed in their phones, seeking interaction and connection; this sight, once mundane, now instills fear in me and stirs questions within my heart.

"I must find balance in my life before I pass away." I muttered decisively to myself.

I remember the first time I left home watching my parents taking leave. "Goodbye, Eleanor," My mother's voice cracked, a delicate tremor betraying her stoic facade. "Take care of yourself, and don't forget to call me." My father stood a silent sentinel, his eyes a mirror of the pride and concern warring within him. As my mother clung to him, seeking solace, I memorized the tableau — a snapshot of unconditional love and the safe harbor I was leaving behind.

I was born and grew up in Edinburgh, Scotland. It wasn't just a city; it was a magnet masterpiece, turning everyone's soul who visits it into an iron halo; a place where history and modernity intertwined in perfect harmony. The sounds of bagpipes echoed through the narrow alleyways, mixing with the chatter of locals and the laughter of tourists, inviting the soul to lose itself in the enchanting allure. With each step, I felt the heartbeat of the city, a pulsating rhythm that drew me deeper into its embrace.

However, life was very quiet there, filled with routine, contrary to what we were taught, "Routine is the sharp sword that cuts between opportunities and creativity." Nevertheless, my ambitions surpassed what this city has offered me. I always had the enthusiasm to seek more opportunities beyond the environment I was raised in. The cobblestone streets and the looming castle were the backdrop of my youth, a canvas of memories painted with the hues of tradition and the whispers of generations past.

Feeling misunderstood by others can be confusing and frustrating, leading to feelings of isolation and emotional turmoil; and that's what happened to me indeed. After all the accusations that were made against me and the harsh words I heard at an early age, I felt as if the world had darkened before my eyes and the sun had extinguished despite its bright light. I was having the sense of not belonging in this city, a stranger in my own homeland, longing for a place that doesn't dig into my identity even if there is a homeland in my heart that never dies, and loyalty in my conscience that endures.

How many nights did I spend searching for the partner while the rain poured heavily outside my window, and the sounds of thunder echoed in the distance? Yet, I didn't pay much attention to the roaring storm outside the window. My thoughts wandered in the realms of imagination, narrating stories woven from the threads of reality and dreams. So, Strong nerve-calming agents were my sole comfort during those tough times when the hour of despair arrived, particularly in those quiet moments of solitude, remembering that I will never surrender my heart to another, no matter what the future holds. This is a decision born out of bitterness or resentment, but also a silent acknowledgment of a reality that I have come to accept. Love, in its many forms, will no longer be a part of my journey.

Yet, there was a part of me that yearned for the unknown, for the sprawling chaos of a metropolis that could challenge the boundaries of my world. Only the unknown road leads to the exploration of new things, and London called to me for that, not with the sophisticated melodies of piano instead of bagpipes, but with the siren song of opportunity and the promise of a new stage upon which to cast my story. It was the piano's promise of a new rhythm, a different harmony to accompany the next chapter of my story.

Finally, after packing my last bag of belongings with trembling hands, I stood by the cage's door, hesitating whether to take the mask that the voices of the bullies deprived me of, or leave it just like I left all my dreams behind. So, I bid farewell to that cage of my upbringing, the room which I always felt in my childhood was prison me of freedom. But after everything that happened, it became the only one that grants me inner peace..

It was time to weave the threads of my destiny in such a bigger place, where people don't care about what others do, in a city where the skyline was a mosaic of ancient and futuristic, where every corner held a different narrative, and every face told a story of its own. That city was London, which calling out to me not with the piano rhymes instead bagpipes, but by the diversity of instruments it offers from all over the world. Perhaps I will find my own group there.

Therefore, I decided to bury my sorrows within my smiles and carry my secrets in my heart. So that my news becomes forgotten within the walls and alleys of the city where I once lived....and begin the journey of crawling from fear, laden with pain and hope, towards a new horizon, away from the confines, to a place where my wounded flesh merges with my pure, clear spirit.

# Chapter 2

It was a summer that year; I arrived in England with ironclad ambitions and wishes. In the labyrinth corridors of London city airport, I took my first step towards the planned unknown. The air swirled with emotions, painting the scene with hues of anticipation and fleeting moments of stress.

Amidst these crowds, there was a precise blend of scents that melded together to create a unique fragrance, presented by the aroma of freshly brewed coffee emanating from the nearby cafes, infused with the sea breeze drifting through the windows, along with the sweetness of fruit-flavored candies, making it refreshing and appealing.

Soon, it was overshadowed by a bouquet of flowers and the freshness, spreading from the cleaning materials; accompanied by the scent of car exhaust and the red brick colour that stubbornly attempts to penetrate the walls, which composed a unique heart for the fragrance.

Finally, she settles on a base of her mood with the scent of airplane fuel, reminding us of its movement from the east, carrying notes of oud and sandalwood, while the other coming from the west is laden with Tonka bean and tobacco.

"Taxi...Taxi."

Where are you headed? The taxi driver voice as he adjusted his Burberry cap with a distinctive checkered pattern made from soft fabric, featuring a rounded crown and a stiff bill projecting in front. He was also dressed in a dark jacket over another layer of clothing.

"To The Draycott Hotel, please," I replied.

Alright, mate! Heading to The Draycott Hotel, yeah? Sit back and relax; we'll get you there in no time," the taxi driver said cheerfully.

"The Draycott, is it?" he mused, eyeing me through the rearview mirror. "You on holiday or is this a permanent move?"

It's a bit of both," I confessed, my gaze fixed on the passing city lights. "A new chapter, you could say."

"New chapters, eh?" he chuckled, navigating the congested streets with ease. "London's full of those. What brings you to our neighbourhood?"

"I'm here to pursue dreams that outgrew my old life," I declared, a mix of determination and apprehension in my tone.

"Dreams!" he nodded, his voice taking on a more serious note. "Just remember, it's not just the dreams that count. It's the will to make 'em real. You got that will, Miss?"

"More than you know," I affirmed, meeting his eyes in the mirror. "And please, call me Eleanor."

While on the way to Chelsea, the outlines of the city began to emerge, one after another, and the driver pointed out its landmarks, even though I hadn't asked him to. However, the charm of the towering castles from ages past did not curb his desire to talk about them as if narrating them for the first time. His words were concise and profound, carrying eloquence in their meanings.

"Here we are, I wish you success," he said, and drove off in his black car, having just added fertilizer to my previously planted aspirations.

I spent the first two weeks swimming through the city's alleyways, as we looked at each other with shyness and affection. In a time where modesty is no longer a virtue, I found myself sinking into the sea of audacity, like a star shining and fading in the darkness.

Day by day, I explored and learned from the challenges of living alone in my apartment in the city center, until I settled in. My financial situation was good, as I worked for a leading company in the field of technology development. I didn't have many friends except for a few colleagues at work.

Reading books was my best friend through the free times, or strolling with my neighbor's young son, Adam, whom I sometimes took with me for shopping; Or simply staying at home, with my Bengal cat tuning in to National Geographic Wild.

On one cold winter night, I sat in front of the fireplace, seeking some warmth from its flames. To my right was my bookshelf, filled with dozens of books. I noticed an old volume with a blue cover, reading it had always brought me joy, but time had not been on my side. In that moment, I felt as though the books were reproaching me: "The constraints of time cannot prevent you from reading me."

I opened the book to a random page and began reading. The book was a culmination of the author's insights gleaned throughout his scientific journey.

I stood there astonished at how Ibn Hazm encapsulated this life in one axis, one end positive and the other negative. The positive side is represented by greed. Greed encompasses all that drives humanity.

Thus, the lover does not love their beloved except out of greed for what they possess... Here, I paused and closed the book, as if I had had my fill of this dose that flowed like a drink into my veins until it mingled with my blood. And so, the idea became like a stream flowing through my mind along with the flow of blood."

After that night, something changed in me. As I listened to people's words, I couldn't shake the feeling that beneath their surface lay a single underlying motive: 'greed.' Even the most innocent greetings, like 'Good morning,' carried an unspoken desire for something more.

James and I, Our relationship was brief.

He was a seasoned employee in the company, where he worked diligently and had good relationships with managers. He was known for his quick wit and helpful nature. We started as colleagues, and then gradually, we broke down the barriers of shyness between us.

Chelsea, T.D department.

James, leaning against the doorframe with a smirk: "What's up with you?" James asked intently, concern evident in his voice. "You seem to be having a bit of bother."

"I'm looking for the company's internal law document," I replied, while scanning through all the papers hanging on the wall.

"Are you after a copy of the company's internal regulations?" he offered.

I nod my head.

"Don't waste time, I'll send you a copy, just give me your email address." James offered, already pulling out his phone.

"I'm Eleanor."

"Nice to meet you mate," James replied with a friendly nod.

...

Later that day, sitting in my room, I found myself still pondering the regulations and how I could better organize them. I wondered if James had already sent the document. So, I messaged him:

Me: "Hi James, I hope you didn't forget the copy."

James: "I didn't, just one moment.

Feeling relaxed now, or still chasing those trivialities?" James quipped, accompanied by a smiling emoji pops up on my screen.

"I responded with a single angry emoji."

"When I need help, don't hesitate to lend a hand," he emphasized."It's a file full of cobwebs. Do you know I haven't read it in years?"

I took a deep breath and managed a small smile. "If you're ever in trouble, let me know. Thanks for helping me out."

James: "No worries. It's good to have someone who takes the company rules seriously; Keeps the rest of us in line."

Me: "I just like to be thorough. But I'm learning that sometimes you need to look beyond the paperwork."

James: "Exactly! And if you ever get stuck, remember, I'm just an email away. No cobwebs in my inbox!"

I couldn't help but laugh, the tension easing from my shoulders: "I'll remember that. Thanks, James. See you tomorrow."

"Oh, wait, I'm heading to Jones's eatery. If you're hungry, don't hesitate to come along—the bill's on you."

My stomach growled as I heard the word 'eatery', so I didn't hesitate for a moment to accept the invitation; but I was also looking for an illusory lust, hoping it might quench my thirst. I grabbed my coat and bag, before I knew how I found myself at Jones's eatery doorstep facing James's open arms. He took me to a secluded table upstairs, just me and him, and the waitress who left soon after taking notes.

"It seems we are all alone" I said softly.

"Yeah, that's why I love this place" he replied, his hand placed on mine.

My body trembled as his touch sent shivers through me. I instinctively pulled away, avoiding his gaze, my cheeks flushing with embarrassment.

Inwardly, I pondered if I had misjudged, attempting to rectify the situation. With a fib, I granted myself another chance. "I believe we're jumping ahead of events," I said flirtatiously, pretending.

"Perhaps, such is our reality, to be or not to be," he replied, extending his hand under the table and gently pressed on my knee.

Then he came closer to me and said, 'I always dreamt of this privacy with you; the company chatter never gave us a chance.'"

He came closer and closer, holding my hands, pressing his forehead against mine, waiting for a kiss that might come from me. I won't hide it from you; for the first time, I felt an indescribable disgust and revulsion. I couldn't hold myself back and bolted towards the bathroom.

The fault wasn't with James; he was handsome, charming, funny, and lacked nothing in terms of masculinity. But the problem was within me and my soul, which rejected any relationship that clashed with its essence and nature. I had known and experienced this many times before, but I ignored the truth and kept searching for a friend who shares even one percent of my nature with me. And I thought James was that person.

I offered him my apologies and tried to explain things in the hope that he would understand. And he did, with a gracious heart. This only strengthened our relationship which developed over time, like a seedling growing into a sturdy tree.

At first, I wasn't sure if what I felt for him was just friendship or something more. Emotions tangled and knotted within me, leaving me uncertain and hesitant. His trivialities only were what moved my previously aching emotions; this made me find solace in him.

In spite of my prior knowledge that this relationship never materializes, I preferred him above all, solely for his foolishness, especially his howling like a wolf for no reason.

As days turned into weeks and weeks into months, the boundaries between friendship and love became increasingly blurred. And then, one ordinary day, the truth hit me like a ton of bricks, stark and undeniable. It was a moment of clarity amidst the chaos of my thoughts, revealing what my heart had known all along.

James was married!!! At that moment, I felt both a sense of relief at our parting and sorrow at losing him. Yet, there were times when he would playfully praise my blue eyes, mixing compliments with jest, which left me feeling uncertain to make a final decision.

Two years pasted in Chelsea, I moved to the heart of London, where there was a branch of the company in need of experienced developers. The offer was presented to me by the manager. There, I met the branch manager, Lori Falheaden, and quickly developed a friendship and a bond with her, especially when she learned that I wasn't involved with anyone and that I live alone with my pet.

She looks gorgeous and fantastic, possessing all the leadership qualities. Even men were intimidated by her, or rather, they dare not approach her. I still hold onto every detail of her features.

As she addressed her team, her gaze was unwavering and her tone commanding, leaving no room for doubt. She expected nothing less than excellence.

Her lips curved into a wide grin, stretching from ear to ear, and her eyes sparkled with warmth. The room seemed to brighten as her smile spread, easing any tension and inviting camaraderie among her colleagues. She would end the meeting with a broad smile followed by a twinkle in her beautiful eyes, under Bangs - Mid Length Haircut to the extent that I didn't know if the attendees were applauding her for her advice or for her captivating presence.

I'd observe the conversational techniques she employed, dissecting them until I could incorporate them into my own personal interactions.

Her dazzling persuasion style was certainly the best thing about her, after her innocent beauty of course.

"Hip the lips, flicked the eyes, and then moaned with a broad smile." That's was her secret...

However, the situation at work quickly deteriorated. Some began secretly accusing me of being mentally ill, while others labeled me as introverted. This caused me significant distress, so I decided to resign from my position after speaking with Lori.

"London City TD."(Technology development department)

Eleanor stood before Lori's office door, waiting for permission to enter, as Lori was engaged in a conversation during a webinar...

Eleanor's gaze fixed on a painting hanging on the right wall. "Come in," Lori signaled with her hand, raising her eyebrows in a gesture of welcome.

"What a beautiful painting!" Eleanor exclaimed, her eyes bright with admiration.

"Yes, it's my favorite animal," Lori replied with a smile, her admiration evident in her expression.

"I love its determination and agility."

Lori leaned back in her chair, crossing one leg over the other, mirroring the posture of the cheetah in the painting:

"I've always been captivated by cheetahs." she added.

Eleanor got excited, feeling a connection forming over their shared admiration for cheetahs.

"Absolutely, they are the ultimate sprinters."

The precision of the details in the picture made Eleanor approach it to examine it closely, while the confusion was clearly visible on her face.

"And their grace! It's a shared interest then. The symbolism varies from one society to another, some see it as a symbol of strength and independence due to its ability to hunt and survive alone."

"Only you could truly symbolize that deep, majestic purple background with such a beautiful face." Eleanor whispered to herself, pondering the enigmatic details of her face with a sense of enchantment.

"Hunt and survive alone ..." Lori asserted as she stood up from her revolving chair. "That's what I called you for"

"I understand that you're going through a tough time, and I heard about your resignation. I'm truly sorry. But don't lose hope, Eleanor, because I have a special offer for you." Lori expressed sympathy for Eleanor.

"No need to apologize. I've been through this before. It's me who should apologize." "What is this offer?"

"I wanted to invite you to join our new women's association."

My eyes widened, eyebrows arching upward, and my mouth formed a perfect 'O' of astonishment.

"What is all about?"

"Sounds like a girls' club! »

"Wow that sounds wonderful! What sorts of things do you focus on?"

«Everything about women! From career development to health and wellness, we've got you covered, all with a big smile on our faces."

With the speed of lightning, I made the decision.

"Count me in! I'm excited to be a part of such a positive community."

"Fantastic! We can't wait to welcome you with open arms!"

"At the end of the week, come round to my place so we can finalize the membership contract and discuss the association's work plan."

"I hope to be helpful."...

I always believe that trying new things, sometimes can lead to unexpected opportunities where you can make a difference. This time, the instinct of greed moved within me automatically. The greed to become a completely independent woman and it is as if the spirit of the cheetah has possessed me.

Clara claimed: "we need to attract more members, my dear."

"Yes, but after finishing framing the association's council members." Lori insisted.

Clara chimed in, "Absolutely! Maya, the lawyer from California, is very excited, as well as Katie Butler, a member of the Senate."

"It seems easy for you guys, indeed!"

"Yeah, indeed."

"You could collaborate with local businesses for events," Clara suggested. "It would increase our reach and support the community."

"Sounds great," Lori said."Our interactions shape our lives, and this initiative could make a real difference."

"A snippet of Clara's conversation from Manhattan via video call before Eleanor enters the office."

# Chapter 3

Hampstead Heath, London, Lori's home.
In the room overlooking the river, Lori reclines on the couch, her thoughts wandering as she absentmindedly runs her fingers through her hair. The silky green Boho Kimono robe cascades gracefully over her voluptuous body, highlighting her beauty and femininity as if woven from golden dreams.
When she shifts softly on the couch, the smoothness of her white thighs catches the eye, glistening like alabaster, or maybe a large piece of Pyreneans white chocolate sculpted by Renaissance artists with hands of silk.

"Ding-dong..." The maid calmly states, "Please come in, Eleanor. She's in the sunroom."
Once Eleanor entered, Lori wasted no time, saying, "Our association needs an unprecedented advertisement to gather the largest number of members worldwide; our friends in America are doing an amazing job, and we should follow suit."
"Awesome," Eleanor replied, "I'll let the advertising manager know and ask her to create a new ad for our page."
"Great, but I didn't mean that, but this," Lori said, as she stood up, provocatively tracing her fingertips over her body and squeezes her breast.

Eleanor could only clamp her jaw shut and arch her eyebrows in a blend of astonishment and perplexity.

"Women's involvement isn't our concern," Lori asserted, "But the support of the affluent is," she echoed, nodding in agreement.

"And that's why they say: 'The right man in the right place.'"

"Do you mean... me?" Eleanor responded with complete spontaneity.

"You're so naïve, Eleanor, are you a man?" Lori's lips quirked in a playful smirk.

"Oh. I'm sorry if I didn't get the hint." Eleanor replied, her cheeks flushing slightly.

"Never mind dear, I'll let you know the outlines of your mission. But after we get ourselves a drink" Lori said, gesturing towards the bar in the elegant lounge where they sat.

After a brief pause, the gentle clink of glass resonated through the room, the maid announced, "Your drink, madam."

"Thanks, Lucy. You can leave now."

As Lucy left, the soft echo of the door closing vibrated, as if it were a romantic melody playing a subtle reminder for the two figures who now found themselves alone with their secrets.

Lori's thigh was now almost entirely visible through the slit of her kimono, revealing her pubic area. This deliberate display was a distraction from the seriousness of her words. The constant flow of the river served as a reminder of the passage of time, of the decisions that had been made, and that could not be undone, much like the waters of the river.

Lori leaned against the window, musing aloud, 'Do these men really care about our association? Certainly not. Everyone has their own agenda. And remember, men hear with their eyes more than with their ears,' she added, and Eleanor was all ears for her.

Eleanor acknowledged," Yes, I know. It's all about greed."

"I admire your intelligence, that's why I told you 'the right man in the right place' and not on social media. So you should be in the right place Elly."

" Any suggestions!" Eleanor inquired.

"Eleanor, at the Wondworth Club, you'll find plenty of targets. All the support is concentrated there." Lori explained.

"Really? How do you know? And how can I get there" Eleanor asked, stopping mid-sip of her juice.

Lori assured, "Trust me, I've scoped it out. It's a goldmine for opportunities." She came near Eleanor and gently held her shoulders. Eleanor nodded, agreeing, "Certainly! I'll make an effort to pop in from time to time."

"We have finalized the contract with Wondworth authorities," Lori announced. "They have given us the green light to set up a women's forum in the first block. Despite its small size, it'll serve its purpose and provide a proper platform for us ladies to exchange ideas."

She recoiled slightly, then picked up her glass again.

"Wow, this is amazing! There will be a forum for us in this luxurious place!"Eleanor exclaimed.

"Yeah, all thanks to Mrs. Clara, the wife of the company's manager." Lori replied. "Next month will be the big day for voting on the forum president. Don't sweat it, we've pretty much all agreed it's going to be you."

"Me!" Eleanor's face lit up with surprise and joy.

"There aren't many candidates, and none of them are enthusiastic."
"You're the only one with a genuine smile among the candidates."Lori added.

"Oh, thank you Lori! I'm truly honored by your trust," Eleanor exclaimed, her eyes shining with gratitude. "Well, the right person in the right place, right?"

"I'll make sure to represent everyone's voice in the forum. Thanks again for believing in me." She added earnestly, with a warm smile. "Loads of potential targets; consider it my gift to your social life." Lori offered with a playful smile.

In reality, there were plenty of candidates, but the online voting system was manipulated in favor of Eleanor to receive 70% of the votes; but who cared about such an unpaid position, after all?

...

After the leaves had fallen and the northern winds began to blow, carrying with them cold breezes one after another, announcing the arrival of winter, our association intensified its training courses for women in various fields.

I also obtained a good schedule at the association, allowed me to balance my private life and contribute to organizing the association's affairs, all thanks to Mrs. Lori's management.

There were several training courses on self-development and independence from men, in addition to teaching the principles of the association to the new members.

Every day, we needed to buy extra chairs until we decided to purchase a large hall to be the venue for our monthly meetings, and the choice fell on the district of Belgravia. Lori was well-planned in what she did.

As for the financial matters of the association, I was not aware of them except in some cases when Lori mentioned that the majority of the contributions came from America.

At 9:00 AM on Monday, the forum was inaugurated with the presence of logos from major companies supporting the event

displayed in a coordinated manner, serving as a clear indication of the association's strength and influence.

It wasn't a large opening due to the venue's privacy, but luxury and extravagance were undeniably prominent. Invitations were extended only to prominent figures in England and some guests from abroad.

The black tinted cars began to converge one by one on the adjacent courtyard to the forum, adorned with natural paving stones, giving it a luxurious and elegant decorative appearance. What enhanced the beauty even further was Lori's welcoming smile near the Forum's entrance, adding a graceful touch as she greeted the delegations.

'Good morning, Mr. Mayor. Please come in,' said Lori, welcoming the attendees one after another.

I didn't know any of them, a fact that heightened my nervousness. It was the first time I met political figures and major investors. But soon, I caught my breath and adapted to the situation, realizing in the end they are just humans like us, or perhaps not as intimidating as I had imagined, or maybe it was a strange feeling that I struggle to put into words.

After a couple of minutes, everyone settled into their seats, and Lori's opening remarks set the tone.

---

'Ladies and Gentlemen, Honored Guests.

Welcome to the hallowed halls of the Wondworth Club, where today we mark not just an event, but a milestone in our journey towards empowerment and excellence.

Although this forum is exclusive to women, its doors remain open to embrace all members of society without exception. Your opinions and viewpoint continue to be highly valued and welcomed in our discussion.

With the esteemed Mayor of London among us, we are reminded of the strength that unity brings. Our collaboration is a beacon of progress, shining across cities and hearts alike.

As we begin, let us channel the warmth of our community to kindle the fires of change. Together, we stand on the cusp of a new era.

Thank you, and let us commence...

In her speech, Lori elucidated the founding principles that drive the organization's mission, emphasizing its purpose with clarity and addressing the myriad challenges that women face worldwide. She highlighted the significant challenges women encounter—gender inequality, violence, and the persistent lack of representation in leadership roles. "We strive to create a global network of support and advocacy..." An excerpt from her speech.

Later on, everyone chats to the tune of soft music, exchanging business cards and engaging in informal networking.

Lori put her arm around Eleanor's shoulder, and whispered in her ear; her facial expression suggesting mischievousness as she poised to address her «Remember they're pretty self-centered, so you gotta play the game. Don't be all sweet and polite; a little sarcasm and rudeness can pique their interest. And keep 'em guessing by playing hard to get. It's all about keeping them on their toes."

Eleanor straightened up, a confident smirk forming on her lips as she met Lori's gaze. 'Trust me, I'm not easy prey,' she replied, her voice steady and assured."

"I wish the party hadn't ended; it was such an enjoyable time."

"Yeah, it really was."

"Please, miss." He offered, extending a glass towards her.

"Oh, I apologise, I don't drink alcohol."

He was a young man in his thirties, somewhat dark-skinned, of medium height, with a slicked-back crew cut hairstyle.

"I notice all the forum workers are female; congratulations on your success."

"It's just the beginning, so stay cautious." She answered him with a laugh.

Then suddenly he dropped the cup he had been holding in his hand. Eleanor was startled, but she reacted quickly and caught the cup before it hit the ground. Her eyes widened briefly in surprise at the sudden drop; however, she quickly regained her composure, showing determination in her focused expression.

Meanwhile, Henry watched with a mix of relief and admiration, his eyebrows slightly raised and a faint smile forming on his lips as he witnessed Eleanor's quick reaction.

Then he broke the silence. Without prior apology, he introduced himself, "By the way, I'm Henry."

"Pleasure to meet you, Henry"

"To be honest, I'm quite chuffed that it's all wrapped up. I didn't know many people here." Henry admitted, the relief evident in his relaxed posture and the faint smile playing on his lips amidst the hum of voices and the occasional clinking of glasses in the forum.

I pretended as if I knew all the guests; Now and then, a nod here, a smile there, greeting everyone I don't know.

"Now that you know someone, you can calm down. No need for breaking cups!"

"I promise I will not, but shall we pop out for a short walk?" There's something I need to show you; it's important." Henry suggested, his voice carrying a hint of urgency, seizing the preoccupation of others with the event.

"I'm not sure Henry, why the secrecy?"

"Because there's something about you; you seem different." Henry replied cryptically.

"Um, What if it's something I'm not ready for?"

"I understand your hesitation, but sometimes the unknown holds the answers we seek. Take a chance, Eleanor. I'll be waiting."

"I understand, but I think I need to stay here to finish organizing everything."

Take all the time you need, but remember, sometimes the biggest discoveries comes from facing our fears head-on."....He said, raising his hand to signal the seriousness "Not everything is as it seems, Eleanor."

Eleanor said tentatively, "I-I'm not sure I understand."

With intense eye contact, he drew very close to Eleanor, breathing in her scent as though trying to study her essence. Leaning in, he murmured, "I'll give you a riddle. If you solve it, call me."

Eleanor remained unfazed, reassured by Henry's non-threatening demeanor. She briefly shut her right eye and shrugged, asking, "Alright then, what is it?"

"The riddle consists of a single word: 'THROV." he explained.

She already knew the answer, yet she was completely stunned; she pretended to be surprised and then asked, "Is it 'TROVE'?"

Henry laughed so hard that he spat out the water, saying" Yeah, it is a 'trove'; pfff"

He continued to stare at her intensely before leaving, handing her a business card with letters "T-H-R-O-V" written on the back. He greeted her with a military salute from afar, then added, "Don't call me if you fail"

She sat there with her mouth agape, unable to respond or say a word. She flipped the card over, reading the spelled-out letters of the hidden word, her expression showing confusion yet filled with hope and curiousity.

"How could all of Lori's advice just vanish in an instant? Not even a single one! That's impossible," Eleanor whispered; her voice tinged with deep dismay and regret.

Approaching the end of this special event, Lori handed the microphone to billionaire Thomas to deliver a closing word of thanks and appreciation to all the esteemed attendees.

"Let's enjoy together moments of joy and reflection before bidding farewell to this wonderful day. Frankly, you added elegance and charm with your gracious presence to enliven the golf club, so we hope you won't deprive us of your attendance every month and add a touch of elegance and femininity to these beautiful moments. Also I invite my friends to join us in organizing competitive tournaments between us and them on the golf course..."

The event was highly successful, as attendees were leaving in comfort under the seductive crimson glow of the Forum's light. While Eleanor reclined in the center, surrounded by the U-shaped arrangement of sofas wandering what Henry had said to her, she closed her eyes for a moment, curiosity with astonishment tickling her mind about the meaning of the cryptic message he had whispered for her.

Then she leaned back against the crimson blanket, pausing for a moment and recalling her childhood memories in Edinburgh. She hesitated between contacting Henry or honoring the promise she made to herself, whispering, 'It's truly a betrayal.

How can I forget Jagger, who suffered because of his love for me? Without me, he wouldn't have suffered as he did.

She continued in this state, her eyes remaining awake until dawn broke, and sleep overtook her.

Around ten in the morning, amongst the clatter of people's shoes and their whispers, Eleanor woke up with an immediate decision planted in her head.

Yes, she decided to contact Henry later, to unveil the curtain of what he is hiding, while she closed all the love outlets in her heart, through which anyone could sneak.

# Chapter 4

After ten months passed... The phone rang.

"Hello," a man's voice talking, tinged with authority.

"Listen carefully, the partners and donors will meet on Saturday to discuss the progress of the project. Make sure to adhere to the specifications they all requested. Okay!"

"Everything is fine."

"I'm glad to hear that! Farewell for now."

The caller said, ending the call abruptly.

...

Time seemed to accelerate, and London's streets soon buzzed with a new energy and hope. Advertising posters were hanging all over London with a big slogan:

"Body, Choice, Life."

"Welcome to Our Big Family!"

This was the association's advertising campaign aimed at attracting the largest number of members, which culminated in tremendous success in record time.

With membership exceeding hundreds of thousands, women from every corner of the globe embraced it passionately. From bustling cities to remote villages, the campaign's message resonated deeply, igniting a wave of enthusiasm and empowerment among women worldwide.

"The advertisement was incredible, Eleanor, you truly are remarkable." Lori praised.

Eleanor replied, "Let's not forget, we spent weeks designing it together." Then she inquired, "Have any notable figures from Belgravia joined us?"

"Indeed, many from the embassies.

"Excellent. Their involvement will be of great assistance."

Then Lori interjected"Oh, I forgot to mention, what you think about conducting a survey among the members?

"Sounds great; it could really enhance our understanding of the members."

"Yeah, understanding their perspectives is crucial for effectively prioritizing discussions on women's aspirations."

Eleanor paused for a moment, deep in thought, and then confidently volunteered: "I'll take on the job survey. I've got this."

"Alright, I'll contact Emma. You can benefit from her expertise in this field."

...

Eleanor sat at her desk, papers scattered around her, eyes fixed on the computer screen. She navigated between books, reviewing questions, adding notes here and there. Emma, the psychological expert, was beside her, pointing out important points with expertise and precision. They exchanged ideas and engaged in passionate discussions throughout the week until it was done. Eleanor looked at Emma with a tired but satisfied smile and said, "Finally, the survey is ready."

The project allocated significant funds to promote itself online, partnering with specialized companies that offer platforms for survey creation, management, and data analysis.

---

Holy creek Miami USA. 04:30 Pm.
The sun shines brightly over the Creek, casting a warm, golden hue across the landscape. The temperature reads 88°F (31°C), but the high humidity, around 66%, makes it feel more like 93°F (34°C). This high humidity attracts people towards shaded and refreshing areas, for comfortable breathing, and enjoys the warm heaviness of the air, that clings to the skin.

The Holy creek is a manmade island, born from the ambition of a billionaire's vision, and stands as a marvel of human ingenuity amid Miami's waters.

The gentle breeze coming from the Atlantic refreshes the warm weather, making it more comfortable to be outside and allowing for clear views of the beautiful surroundings. This intimate atmosphere, with all its expressions, awaits anyone who unleashes its desire to be carried away by its warm breezes.

---

The island, often hailed as the eighth wonder of the world,- while I'm not sure if any wonder held that title before it- stand as a testament to unparalleled creativity and astonishing craftsmanship. Its design lines and the fragrant colors of the gardens seamlessly blend wilderness with civilization, reality with imagination, thereby leaving no chance to any other design take its place.

More than an island surrounded by blue beaches and towering palm trees, but a luxurious resort that boasts the finest facilities and gardens, which have long been discussed in legends and embodied by visionary billionaire's dream ; especially the flow of water that you stand in awe of, whether it's flowing above or streaming beneath your feet.

"I'm heading out, dear. Don't forget to feed the cat." Dame Evelyn Sterling stated.

"Don't worry baby; I'll make sure she's fed... Enjoy your time! I'll call Henry to make sure he fulfills your request." The billionaire husband replied.

"Oh honey, you're nasty" Dame Evelyn Chuckled.

Under the majestic palm trees, with the sun's rays reflecting off the meticulously designed pool, Rebecca basked in the warmth of Miami from her villa.

She reclined on a chaise lounge by the expansive pool, surrounded by the beauty of Rosa Mundi roses, ferns, and a perfectly manicured grassy floor that completed the tranquil scene. Facing the towering marble pillars that led to the villa's interior, she felt a profound sense of peace and luxury.

---

The delicate scent of the Rosa Mundi roses mingled with the refreshing aroma of the water and lush greenery, creating a tranquil and sophisticated ambiance. It was the perfect setting for Rebecca to unwind and savor the beauty of her surroundings.

"Dear Rebecca, you always shine! Thomas is lucky to enjoy your beauty." Evelyn greeted her warmly.

---

Rebecca sighed, "Ah, that arrogant one, nothing impresses him," she replied, gently stroking her dog with a delicate hand.

---

Evelyn turned to the dog and asked with concern, "Felix, does mommy take good care of you?

---

Felix barked happily, as if affirming, "Yes."

---

"Poor Felix, indeed he's feeling trapped in this prison." Rebecca said with bitterness.

---

"The same goes for Katie; the authorities oppose this! What can we do?" Evelyn lamented.

"If only we were in Virginia," Rebecca mused.

---

"There are plenty of beauties there; you could meet one of them," Evelyn suggested, stroking Felix.

Felix lay on his front paws, his short tail wagging with a faint hope of adventure.

"Ah, I almost forgot why I came here. I've convinced my husband to join his friend in buying a new island. You can join us. This time it will be entirely self-governing for us." Evelyn suggested to Rebecca.

Rebecca's eyes sparkle with optimism, reflecting her enthusiasm for the venture "A new island? That sounds incredible, Evelyn! She exclaims eagerly while jumping up from the chaise lounge. "I'm dying to know more; share the details, please."

Evelyn nodded enthusiastically, "Yes, it's a chance for a fresh start, away from all the restrictions. Imagine it, Rebecca – our own paradise."

Felix's tail wagged even faster, as if sensing the excitement in the air. Rebecca smiled, feeling a spark of hope. "Count me in. This could be the adventure we've been waiting for. Looking up at the sky, she imagined herself in their new home, "A place where we can truly be free."

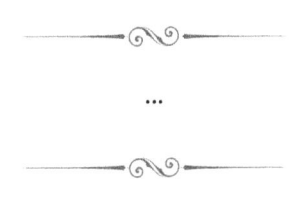

---

...

---

Belgravia, London.

The comprehensive survey was conducted across the UK and some European countries. In response to the finding, Lori appointed an expert women's team to assist a large group of women. Most of the assistance involved legal support or healthcare, particularly for cancer patients and some rare diseases.

All this success stemmed from the survey, which uncovered many of the issues women were hiding during open meetings, enabling outreach to those in need via phone or email.

...

Eleanor stood before the mirror, staring at herself with a keen eye. With deliberate precision, she traced her eyeliner, accentuating her features and highlighting the curves. She selected a pair of tight-fitting jeans that hugged her body and accentuate her figure.

As she looks at herself, she feels confident and attractive, unable to resist a bit of playfulness and flirtation, it's as if today she's rather pleased with herself.

The cropped shirt emphasizes her long legs, and delicate belly button, like a pearl in the middle of her abdomen, showcasing the under average boobs, and her appealing backside. The low-cut neckline, revealed her cleavage and adding a touch of allure and sexiness to her ensemble.

---

Lori had taught her how to harness all this elegance to allure the wealthy at the club; while Eleanor already possessed all these features, with her fair, childlike skin resembling a masterpiece crafted in Sicily, each graceful movement and delicate feature spoke of a natural beauty that drew admiration and envy alike.

At her usual spot on the Wondworth Club's golf course, Eleanor paused, awaiting Sunday morning matches. She appeared relaxed yet confident; with each swing of her club, she effortlessly caught the eye of other members with her smooth moves, making an impression without trying too hard.

However, it seemed that the man's patience had its limits; after seeing her through the building's glass, he couldn't bear struggle of his desires any further, unlike his companions.

"Excuse me, can I ask you a question?" he asked.

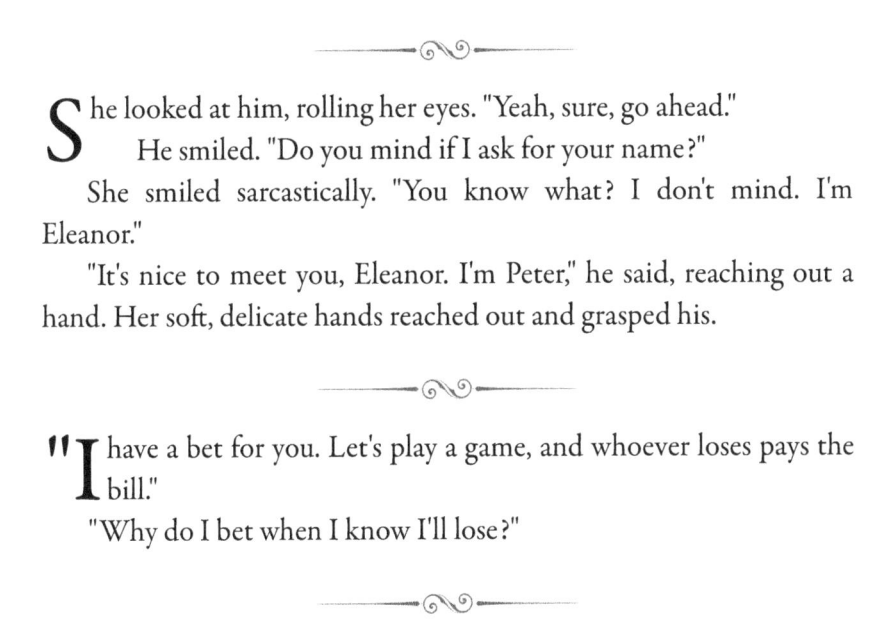

---

She looked at him, rolling her eyes. "Yeah, sure, go ahead."

He smiled. "Do you mind if I ask for your name?"

She smiled sarcastically. "You know what? I don't mind. I'm Eleanor."

"It's nice to meet you, Eleanor. I'm Peter," he said, reaching out a hand. Her soft, delicate hands reached out and grasped his.

---

"I have a bet for you. Let's play a game, and whoever loses pays the bill."

"Why do I bet when I know I'll lose?"

---

He Laughs "You're right, you'll definitely lose. Just look at those skinny arms of yours! It looks like you haven't lifted a weight in your life."

---

"This is my strength," she said, winking.

---

"The green fee's on me, but only if you let me teach you how to score."

"What a gentleman you are! But just so you know, I've made a lot of money, and my deals are quite profitable," she whispered in his ear. "So it's all just a game," she purred, her eyes glinting mischievously.

---

Peter smiled sarcastically again, "Sure, keep telling you that. We'd see who was laughing when you lost, O you indulged one."

---

She smirked, "Sure, I'll take you on a round. It would probably be more fun than what you're doing here. Anyway, what do you say?" She held her hand out to him.

---

"Aw, don't be like that. I'm sure you'll have more fun with me than with this stupid game." He takes her hand and leads her to the golf course.

Usually, it's the man who extends his hand first, but Eleanor's gesture came from complete confidence in what she was doing. She knew exactly where to stand and how to shake hands, raising her right hand confidently to subtly influence him psychologically, unbeknownst to him. She was adept in body language, a skill unfamiliar to many.

And things continued in this manner with Eleanor; she would pick up anyone who tried to pick her up first. With great tact and eloquence, she was able to tame men without establishing an intimate relationship with them; rather, she gained their respect and support for the association, unlike other charming women at the forum who were sent by Lori to the club to assist Eleanor with her mission.

So it became known for its members from every race, whose beauty was unparalleled in the world.

The club was called the Crimson Club.

With all this allure mixed with cunning, emotions became entangled in the forum, turning it into a stage for competition between billionaires and these women. At times, the woman faltered, and at other times, the billionaire headed straight to Belgravia.

Everything Lori had planned succeeded indeed, and the association received intense support, both financially and morally.

09:00 Am

Pablo, the young Billionaire, follows his father's footsteps, Jefferson, the investment mogul in the stock market and owner of real estate companies in both Canada and the USA, with a wealth exceeding $40 billion. Jefferson is known for his deep financial analysis skills and smart decision-making, especially in supporting promising startups.

Pablo, with well defined muscles, was leaning on the barrier overlooking the green grass, uninterested in the match, while browsing his phone. An easy and elegant prey, who could be better than him? He possessed all the qualities any woman could be attracted to: Handsome, elegant, immensely wealthy, and on top of that, kind and fun-loving.

This opportunity couldn't pass unnoticed by Jessica, the gorgeous tiny girl with brown skin, and her friend Lily the slender blonde girl, who gazed at him from afar.

They sipped their margaritas, checking out Pablo," Wow, what a catch," Lily whispered. "The spoiled boy"

Jessica: "Look who we have there, it's the spoiled boy."

Pablo's emerald green eyes amidst his tan skin sparkled as he smiled at them. Made Lily a little flustered, "What a handsome guy."

Jessica: "And filthy rich too. Let's get a bit closer to him,"

Jessica leaned on the barrier near him, unintentionally displaying her charms, while Lily smiled at him and get closer to her.

He responded with a sweet smile, but men always seem to be slow in understanding signals.

"Charming guy, but dim-witted, can't he see what's going on?" Lily whispered to Jessica.

Jessica intensified her hints, winked at Pablo, trying to get his attention. When he finally caught on, she said, "Let's grab a table."

"Let's sit at this table," Lily suggested.

Jessica waved to him from a distance and then sat with Lily.

As they sat down, Pablo walked over and plopped down beside them. They are both feeling a little nervous and excited, but also feeling confident that he is interested in them.

"So, you're golfers, huh?" Pablo asked.

"Uh, nope. Just soaking up some Vitamin D," Jessica replied with a laugh.

"I thought you were golfers, you have all the skills."

The girls laughed, «Skills? Which ones?" Jessica asked.

"I mean charm, Beautiful skirt! You know something like that" then he invited himself to sit down "Mind if I join you guys?"Of course if you're here alone?"

"Actually, we're alone," Lily said. "But yeah, come on down."

Pablo smirked, and sat down. "Don't worry, I don't bite! So, what's your name?" he asked, addressing Jessica.

"I'm Jessica, and this is my friend Lily."

"Hey, nice to meet you both," Pablo said. "I can tell you're not into golf. What do you guys like to do for fun?"

"You're right; we love traveling, relaxing, forming friendships."

"Yeah, it's amazing to be able to explore the world and meet people from all walks of life," Lily added.

"I reckon you two are dead lucky..."

The girls exchanged a look, then shrugged. "Lucky? Yeah maybe, but why's that?"

"Because you get to meet me," Pablo said with a wink.

A few minutes into the conversation, Lily turned to him with a mixture of curiosity and amazement. 'How on earth do you manage to make so much money?' she asked, her tone laced with skepticism.

Jessica chuckled and chimed in, "Yeah, show us the secrets to your success, Pablo!"

Pablo shook his head. "Let me tell you, though, being rich isn't always about being smart; There are plenty of foolish people who are wealthy, and plenty of smart ones who are poor."

"Come on, Pablo, Don't beat around the bush" Jessica said, her tone playful and encouraging.

Alright, alright, let's break it down. Wealth can be divided into two camps: inherited, which is a no-brainer, and acquired. You're asking about the latter, right?

The girls nodded, their ears perked up and focused on Pablo.

"Wealth often follows an easy path, which most people are unaware of it. The first step is the idea: identify what you want to achieve? It's impossible to become wealthy if you don't believe in your idea.

Once you truly believe in your idea, the opportunities start pouring in. That's where the magic happens. Some people seize them, while others remain stuck asleep. It all comes down to boldness and the willingness to take action. Indeed."

Lily whispered to Jessica, "Did we get any of that?"

Jessica shrugged. "Not really" she raised an eyebrow, "And what about you? What do you reckon you're worth, then?"

"Alright, I'm not going to lie, my old man's got the cash, but I'm still building my own empire. I haven't inherited it yet. Ha-ha."

"But you're enjoying it, aren't you?"

Pablo chuckled. "No way, I'm working towards my own wealth.

So, I founded my first company when I was 20, and let me tell you, it was a wild ride. I had only $2,000 to my name and was pretty fed up with my dad at the time. I desperately wanted to break free from his shadow.

As I mentioned earlier, the idea is the most important thing. And honestly, the idea of starting my own business had been gnawing at me for ages. I started researching the market and stumbled upon car shampoo - yeah, you heard that right, car shampoo production! I chatted with my childhood friend, and he was even more stoked than I was. As they say, "believing is seeing. Within days, he went off to ask about the prices of plastic bottles in the city where he was studying, all while we were both clueless about how to make the stuff, but our faith in the idea was stronger than any obstacle. You see, faith in the idea is the key.

The next day, my friend returned looking pretty blown away. He'd asked his cop cousin who works in Orlando if he could tag along with, but the cousin was out sick. Then his cousin remembered another cop buddy who could go with him instead.

My friend said to me, trembling, "I was really scared last night, especially with what you told me." Then he began to narrate the events to me:

So I went along for the ride. On the way to the city, I turned to the guy and asked "I hear a weird bubbling sound in the car trunk."

The cop replied, "Oh, that's just the car shampoo."

"What... car shampoo" I exclaimed in surprise, "Is this guy for real??" as if the idea had shocked or startled me.

The cop said, "Yeah, I make it and sell it to car wash stations. It's all about hustling these days – life's just gotten too expensive."

Pablo said," And that's the thing – Opportunities fall from sky. And here lies the crucial difference between wealth and poverty; you're either bold enough to take the leap or stuck in fear."

Jessica and Lily exclaimed earnestly,"Oh my god!"

Lily let out a wistful sigh and whispered, 'I've always dreamed of becoming a wealthy actress.' Jessica's eyes lit up with shared ambition as she echoed her friend's sentiment: 'me too.'

Pablo's encouragement was unwavering. "Why not, you've got the talent, I told you before, ha-ha. Just trust yourself and believe in it."

"Okay, girls, I've got a proposal for you," Pablo said, his tone casual and inviting. 'Want to come with me on a weekend getaway this Saturday?"

Their hearts race with excitement and trepidation. Jessica, the more pragmatic of the two, spoke up first. "A trip, you say? That sounds great. But I'm not sure we know you well enough."

Pablo's lips curled into a knowing smile "I've told you before, I don't bite"

Lily's eyes sparkled with mischief as she chimed in, "Come on, Jess, it'll be fun! We've been stuck in this routine for ages. A little adventure never hurt anyone."

"I don't know, Lily. This all seems a bit... too good to be true. I'm afraid."

Pablo held up his hands in a calming gesture, his gaze steady on Jessica's. "Your safety and comfort are my top priorities."

After a moment of deliberation, Jessica nodded. ""Okay, Pablo. We'll take you up on your offer. When do we head out?"

The encounter concluded with the exchange of the phone numbers.

---

"The Crimson Forum, 03:00 PM"

Under the crimson red lights, Eleanor took a tablet of SNDRIs and sank into the leather couch with her phone in hand. She called a woman in need of help, identified through the previous survey. Typically, there is a team in Belgravia that makes the calls to women, and rarely did Eleanor contact the identified targets. She focused only on a specific group of individuals, those suffering from acute Therianthropic breakdown.

The day Henry's departure from the forum sparked a great curiosity mixed with nerves and determination in Eleanor. She couldn't resist calling him the next day, hoping that he would answer her questions, or maybe even more than that, with a firm resolve not to have a relationship with him.

That conversation on the opening day seemed like just a few fleeting minutes, but it ignited that longing for the past that had been taken from Eleanor against her will, along with years of internal struggle and the attempt to suppress her feelings. It also heralded a present filled with new opportunities and paths that might be better than the old memories.

On that typically calm Sunday night, Eleanor's psyche revealed a stark contrast. The weekend's tranquility gave way to inner turmoil, charged with emotions. Her phone screen swayed between her fingers, but soon her desire, or rather instinct, overcame reluctance. The privacy of her room encouraged and comforted her, providing the security needed to gather her thoughts.

With a deep breath and heavy sigh, she made the decision to dial his number. Her slender hands fumbled in the darkness of the nightstand, searching for the heavy mask. Slowly, she lifted it and placed it upon her face — a mask she had kept for twelve years, worn whenever she exhausted all patience with sorrow. Alone in her room, unseen and untouched by others, she bore the weight of guilt. Tears flowed silently under this mask, warm and unbidden, soothing her longing for what was lost and calming the tremors of shock. The cheetah mask always made her feel at home.

Meanwhile, the Blackberry ringtone and vibration shook Henry's heart, prompting him to leap from the bed, and answer without letting it breathe. This swift response made Eleanor hold her breath, without saying a word. And so began Eleanor's adventure...

# Chapter 5

"So you solved the riddle," Henry said, visibly relieved after almost losing hope.

"Yeah, I think it's an acronym," she replied, her voice quiet and slightly startled.

---

"Did it really take you that long?" he asked, a mix of curiosity and disbelief in his tone.

---

"You really surprised me! Maybe you mistook me for someone else that day?"

---

"No, I didn't," Henry said.

---

"Only a few people know this acronym, THROV: Transformed Humans Rally Over Varieties. But how did you know this" Eleanor asked.

---

Henry explained, "Sometimes our actions reflect our feelings in a way that doesn't need words."

---

Eleanor acknowledged, "What a keen sense you have!"

---

"Oh, I didn't know I had this sense. I'm a super guesser." Henry said jokingly.

"Hehe, I think so," Eleanor giggled softly.

"You know well, Ely, this isn't your home," Henry stated deeply."
With closed eyes and drawn-in cheeks, tears began to fall beneath the mask as she confessed, "Maybe you don't know, but I've let go of this idea long ago."

"Perhaps ideas can be left behind, but one's personality cannot."

Ellie paused for a moment, lost in her tears.

With great compassion, Henry endeavored to reignite hope once more.

"Don't cry, Ely, everything will be alright. Trust me."

"Or are you saying you won't chase rabbits?" he added with a hint of humor.

She wiped away her tears and burst into laughter, loudly exclaiming with a humorous tone, "I won't!"

After Eleanor felt reassured by Henry's words, she experienced a sense of relief and became more open to conversation. They continued throughout the night, alternating between jest and banter, ultimately arranging to meet the next day.

---

However, in Belgravia, things were not going well, tension hung thick in the air as rumors swirled about illicit activities at the esteemed Wondworth Club. In the rainy dusk, Lori received a private message from the club manager.

Sophie, her devoted assistant, watched anxiously as Lori brow furrowed deeper while reading the message.

"Lori, you really need to see this," Sophie insisted urgently, thrusting the phone towards her. Her nervous energy was palpable, evident in her fidgeting hands and the tightness in her voice.

Lori's eyes widened as she scrolled through the unpleasant series of photos and a video that slowly unraveled a harsh reality.

She played the video, her eyes widened in shock.

A moment of silence followed, broken only by the sound of rain tapping against the window. She struggled to process the disturbing images: a young girl on her knees, her face pale and eyes wide, surrounded by obscured figures, their intertwined legs the only visible detail.

The little lady, smiling shyly in the middle of the crimson Forum, responded to the man's question about her age, her response sending a shiver down Lori's spine. Another man was seated on low, inviting couches scattered with silk cushions; seemed to be engaging with her in a manner that made Lori's skin crawl. Do you like this? The man said through the screen.

She answered with a loud "Yeah," While she tenderly grasped his ...., her fingers wrapped around him, moving with slow, rhythmic motion that brought him to the edge.

The scene took a darker turn as the third man demanded her gesture of gratitude towards the one she loves, grasping her face gazed to the camera. She looked into the lenses, her voice quivered with a mix of emotions as she murmured words of indebtedness "Thank you Lori, for sending me to this place of bliss, I love you" and she blew her a kiss into the air.

That Damning photos and texts revealed a clandestine commercial work ring operating within the club's elegant confines. Lori called the manager; his voice trembled as he recounted stumbling upon this sordid truth, fearing for the club's reputation and the safety of its members.

"The cleaner found the CD outside my office," the manager confessed to Lori, his voice trembling. "I don't usually shy away from things, but seeing that explicit content—I was taken aback. This could ruin us," he added in a barely audible whisper, his concern evident.

Lori took a deep breath, trying to steady her nerves. "This girl has no relation with us. But we can't let this get out. Do you have any idea who might be behind this?" murmured Lori, her mind racing with the implications of their discovery.

Sophie nodded solemnly, fully grasping the gravity of the situation.

They had uncovered a scandal that could shake Belgravia's elite to its core. But revealing the truth was merely the beginning; the real challenge lay in how they would expose it without becoming ensnared in the dangerous web they had uncovered.

---

"I can't believe what's happening, I really can't" Lori said angrily, in a loud voice as she entered her office, with Sophie following closely behind.

"Those insolent ones have indeed gone too far. We must put an end to this," Sophie suggested firmly, slamming her hand on the desk.

Lori grabbed her head, deep in thought, before murmuring, "It's not their fault, it's mine, but soon, I will clarify matters."

Sophie hissed through clenched teeth," I don't know if I can sit with these bitches. You have no idea how angry I am."

Lori asked, "Do you know that young girl?"

Sophie replied curtly, "No."

They are truly clueless; they don't understand independence. I will never stay silent about this. Tomorrow, we will set things straight."

Lori pondered briefly, then as if struck by inspiration, "No, it's not about the women in the forum. There's someone else trying to exert control over us."

...

By the forenoon's brightness and radiant glow, the azure horizon stretched endlessly, sporadically adorned by wisps of clouds. The sun's brilliance only served to enhance its beauty and clarity beyond words. It was indeed a beautiful day, brimming with warmth, awaiting only someone bold enough to embark on a new beginning. And who better than the person who had just awakened from a deep serene slumber, having dreamt of it for so long? Yes, it was the new Eleanor, or rather, the original Eleanor.

A gentle sound of the door handle, accompanied by a soft click of the seatbelt, was followed by the reassuring hum of the engine ready to gear up. Eleanor launched the music through her phone connected to the car stereo before beginning to drive.

As the song began, she pressed her foot down on the pedal.

"How do you do? You like me and I like you. Come and take me by the hand 'cause I wanna be your friend. How do you do? You like me and I like you. Say, ho..." - The music filled the car-

With the vibrations of the loud bass thumping through the speakers, Eleanor drove to the forum as usual, feeling energetic and full stamina. This time, a long-absent smile brightened her face; her hair danced in the wind, and her cheeks flushed with excitement from the powerful Jaguar JXS engine, making her feel reborn. However, this feeling quickly faded once she entered the forum.

On the elevated platform in the middle of the hall, Lori was standing, and the women seated around her on the couches exchanged puzzled looks, their faces confused, indicating their ignorance of the reason for the meeting.

Eleanor entered the forum with a graceful yet hesitant step, her eyes scanning the room for familiar faces. She wore a simple but elegant dress that highlighted her delicate features and calm demeanor.

The other women, each with their unique charm, ranged from the youthful exuberance of Jessica's emerald eyes and quick smile, to the serene wisdom of Sophie, whose silver hair and gentle presence commanded quiet respect.

As soon as everyone had gathered, among them Eleanor, Lori began to reprimand them, But she did not disclose the tragedy that occurred.

"Ladies, I know you're surprised by the suddenness of this meeting, but if it wasn't important, we wouldn't have contacted you or gathered here. After noticing that some of the ladies have been taking advantage of this forum, we decided to convene and discuss this matter.

Firstly, I want you to know that I am not here to meddle in your personal affairs or attempt to undermine your freedom. However, after receiving numerous reports about the actions of some of you, I became deeply concerned, and I cannot deny feeling intense anger. Therefore, I decided to postpone the meeting until today, hoping that the anger would subside."

I know my words today may be unsettling for some, but as the saying goes: 'Tell the truth even if it's bitter.' It's a warning, a realization of the reality we live in. Some men still don't see us as equals, they don't see us as partners, but as pawns to be manipulated and discarded at their whim.

We often find ourselves drawn to sweet words, gentle gestures, and bright smiles, only to quickly realize that they are fake all. Yes, they may stroke our feelings, but it's only for their own desires. They may promise, but they'll never keep. So don't be victims of these wolves in sheep's clothing, who leaving us broken and disillusioned in their wake.

This made me refuse to see my sisters fall victims to these cunning foxes, while I stand idly by. It's time to give ourselves greater value, value yourself; people will value you. Yes, we are strong enough to overcome. Indeed, that's how we should be."

Some of the women started rolling their eyes here and there, each one pretending her surprise and innocence towards the behavior of others. Even Eleanor's face turned red, as if Lori was specifically targeting her.

Meanwhile, Lori continued her speech with heavy steps, moving between the couches: "Believe me; anyone who believes in love stories with the ultra-wealthy is completely mistaken. These individuals have complex intention, you're now glowing candles, but your light will quickly extinguish after the first tremor. This is their reality, yes. And you don't know when it will ignite again in their eyes, maybe a week, a month, or perhaps never.

Sophie interjected, saying: "This is the reality of all men, not just the wealthy."

The women began, one after the other, expressing their views on the matter, alternating between support and opposition. Until they split into three groups: Lori's group, advocating for complete independence from men, treating them merely as tools to serve women, by arousing them only.

The second group prioritized self-interest above all else, with their motto being 'Better to offer my love tunnel on a private jet, tasting champagne, with social benefits in addition, than offer it to someone I love, later then betrays me and leaves me like a fool.

The third group consisted of Eleanor alone, who whispered to herself: 'What disgusting creatures' humans can be.'

Events quickly escalated, and things turned into a hidden internal conflict within the association. Each sought supporters, recruiting as many attractive girls as possible to kill men peacefully.

It was a battle between two enemies, same target, and so their weapons: Arrows hovering posed above brows, red poison gleaming beneath them on their lips, and a shiny hair meticulously styled. All aimed to bring down the victims, compelling them to kneel before bubble butts, and shapely boobies, expertly enhanced with pink nipples creams.

However, the ultimate goal varies between wealth and power, allure and submission. Lori led the first team, focusing on strategic moves to gain influence and control. Her team members were ambitious and driven, each with a clear vision of their path to success. They held meetings in sleek boardrooms, discussing investments, power plays, and the next big move.

On the other hand, Jessica and her friends pursued pleasure and luxury. They often dreamt of exclusive parties, dressed in the latest fashion, and surrounded by opulence. Their gatherings were filled with laughter, indulgence, and the pursuit of enjoyment. Jessica's emerald eyes sparkled with excitement as she and her friends explored new experiences, from exotic vacations to high-end shopping sprees.

Despite their different paths, both groups were united by their determination to achieve their goals, whether it was through power and influence or through pleasure and luxury

After the meeting concluded, everyone left feeling disheartened each determined to stick to their own beliefs. Even Eleanor hurriedly departed like a shooting star, with a pale face, which added to her beauty rarely matched by her peers on this planet. She headed directly to the Kyoto Garden, where she had arranged to rendezvous with Henry.

On the wooden bench overlooking the fish pond, Henry was sitting under the cherry blossom tree, with flickering eyes between sleep and wakefulness, with hands clasped behind the back of the bench, he was listening to the melodies of the birds hidden among the leaves of the trees, sipping his favorite drink, carrot juice.

Until Eleanor unexpectedly attacked him:

"Roar, roar" her voice filled with the ferocity of a hunting predator.

"Oh, shit!" he exclaimed as the cup of juice slipped from his grasp, over his jeans, and he leaped like a frightened rabbit from the seat.

"Aw, I'm so sorry! I didn't think... I'm really sorry!"

"Hahaha! Don't worry! Oh my god, you're really skilled at hunting."

"Let me clean your pants, I've wet wipes."

"Come on, forget about this nonsense. Everything is fine; the important thing is that you're here. How are you doing? »

"I told you, I'm always clumsy and dangerous."

He said, as he turned back and donned the rabbit mask: "This time, you won't get me." Then he hurried away, disappearing into the bamboo forest.

Eleanor looked around, the shyness filled her face, but she couldn't resist. Eagerly, she shifted her hips, ready to hunt. Then she set off on the search journey again. It didn't take long before she caught him, hiding inside the trunk of a giant plane tree in Holland Park.

The pursuit continued amidst the surprise of some visitors, as they paid no heed to anyone. Finally, exhaustion overtook them, and they collapsed onto the grass opposite the rock garden, standing by the tiered waterfall.

"Eleanor! Would you please tell me about yourself? What happened to you? The world has truly changed. Today, there are thousands of Therians. So why did you refuse to acknowledge yourself?"

"If we consider my counterparts, there are millions."

"What do you mean?"

Eleanor was flooded with memories.

Everything began when my sister brought a cat to our home. It was playful, beautiful, and full of energy. It would sleep in my lap all night.

But when she turned 6 months old, stray cats began entering our house searching to mate with her, which annoyed my parents a lot. So they asked me to take her to my aunt's house, which is isolated, built on top of rocky hill. I took her with a broken heart at the thought of leaving her, but knowing I would visit her daily made it bearable. Otherwise, I wouldn't have left her for a moment.

Henry: "I bet you've loved her. What happened next?"

The small cat was placed in a Grocery shopping bag, and Eleanor carried her to aunt's house. She climbed the slope, one step after another, with the ease and agility of children who know no fatigue or weariness. As for the cat, she clung to the bag, silently in bewilderment; Eleanor's promises were pure and innocent: "You're lucky, the garden will be yours alone, and I will come to visit you every day." She continued talking all the way, until she arrived at her aunt's door and entered directly.

"Good afternoon! Mother sent you this stubborn cat for you to take care of" She joked her cousin, who was in her twenties, and was coincidentally in the garden.

"Here, give it to me," he said.

She responded with excitement."There you go, she's beautiful."

He took two steps back, and then rushed four steps forward, with a dry heart and cold blood he threw it from the top of the hill into the neighbor's garden below. The height was about 100 meters.

Eleanor stood frozen; her eyes couldn't believe what they were seeing. The cat, once nestled in the wicker basket, now plummeted through the air like a fragile leaf caught in a gust of wind. She watched as it disappeared over the edge of the hill, its tiny body shrinking into the distance. She peered over the fence into the neighbor's garden, hoping to catch any sign of life. The dense trees within the garden obstructed her view, leaving her with no indication.

"Why?" Eleanor's voice trembled. "Why would you do that?"

"Don't worry; she won't die. Cats have seven lives."

He left, and she left without even saying hello to her aunt. With hurried steps, a shocked psyche, and eyes struggling to hold back tears, she entered the house.

Eleanor's mother: "What did your aunt say to you?"

With a quiet voice, Eleanor responded, "The cat died."

"Died! What are you saying! And How?"

Eleanor entered her room and sat on the bed after closing the door behind her. She didn't speak, she didn't cry, but rather, the image of the floating wicker basket in the sky kept spinning in her mind.

"Oh my God, this person is a criminal," Henry exclaimed.

Eleanor's eyes remained like clouds full of rain, and it didn't rain until the nightfall, when she realized what had happened and that she couldn't protect her. She carried an eternal grudge against her cousin in silence, without a word. She was unable to express her feelings in words, so she chose silence to express the pain within her.

Days passed and Eleanor's state did not change, despite all attempts to convince her to bring another cat. The doctor said she was just shocked by the traumatic incident and will get over it. Until the fifth day arrived, where the father made her an offer:

"This time, I'll bring you a strong animal. You won't need to defend it; on the contrary, it will defend you." The father said it gently with tightly shut eyes, playing the role of a doctor trying to alleviate her burden.

Is it a cheetah? Eleanor spoke, after days of silence."

The father's life regained its vitality after hearing her speak again, and with great interest, he said, 'Yes, how you knew?' he Encouraged her to express her feelings and thoughts.

Eleanor responded by shrugging her shoulders." indicating her uncertainty to answer.

The mother said in a tone of exasperation, "I think you've made things even more difficult. Where will you get a cheetah from?"

"I don't know, but what should I say to her! The important thing is that she spoke, that alone is an achievement."

"Tomorrow, I'll search for a cuddly cheetah. Perhaps I'll find one at the bear factory."

Eleanor chose the cheetah as her spirit animal, along with a meticulously crafted spotted mask. From there, her personality began to crystallize with the cheetah. Her small room became a sanctuary for cheetah images adorning the walls, the TV screen rarely straying from savannah programs, much like the mask that never left her smiling face. Accompanied her to school, where classmates whispered, "Eleanor's the girl with the cheetah mask." They didn't understand—the mask wasn't a mere accessory; it was her alter ego. Beneath its playful exterior lay determination and a promise: She would protect those like her—The Therians—no matter the cost.

Everything was fine, even her friend Jagger, the 11-year-old son of their neighbor, shared the same feeling. Every evening, they would meet to play together on the outskirts of Edinburgh.

Jagger, the neighbor's son, lived in the prominent estate that stood out compared to the modest houses around it. The luxury cars parked out front and the beautifully manicured gardens were a testament to his family's wealth. His pampered upbringing caused his school friends to drift away, unable to relate to his sheltered existence. But Eleanor was different. She paid no mind to his tantrums and spoiled behavior, which oddly comforted him and forged an unlikely friendship between them.

Eleanor's visits became a routine, alternating between her house and his. However, his mother's disapproval of Eleanor was evident. She often cautioned him, hinting at her unease with cautious glances and subtle remarks. Beneath it all, she harbored a sense of superiority; viewing herself as above the ordinary folk, she dismissively called "the poor."

Despite this, their mutual feeling lent strength to their relationship. As they parted, their steps were laden with the weight of longing, yet when they reunited; it was as if they soared on the wings of eagles.

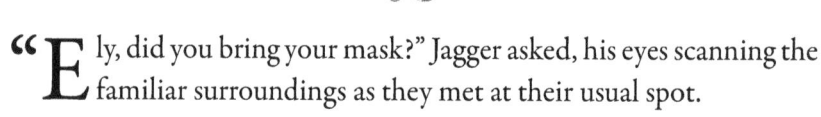

---

"Ely, did you bring your mask?" Jagger asked, his eyes scanning the familiar surroundings as they met at their usual spot.

---

"Of course, Jagger! What about you?" Eleanor replied with a smile, reaching into her bag to show him her mask. She held it up triumphantly, the fabric catching the light.

---

"Awesome! Let's go," Jagger exclaimed, his voice brimming with excitement as he started to run ahead.

But before they could take off, Eleanor called out loudly, "Wait!" Her voice echoed, stopping Jagger in his tracks.

---

"I'm going to chase," Jagger declared, and he dashed across the road toward the Water Leith, his feet pounding the pavement.

---

On the opposite bank of the river, Jagger spotted a rabbit hopping about. He pointed it out to Eleanor, expressing his desire to catch it.

"Let's leave it; it's on the opposite side," Eleanor said, her voice calm but firm.

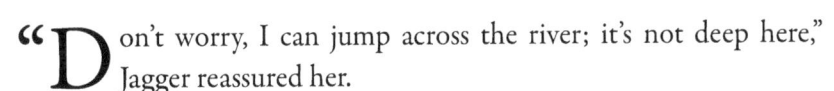

---

"Don't worry, I can jump across the river; it's not deep here," Jagger reassured her.

"Stop, you fool! I won't let you do this. Follow me, I know a beautiful place," Eleanor exclaimed. But Jagger jumped into the river anyway! The river wasn't deep, but he couldn't get out because the current carried him away from Eleanor's sight behind the trees.

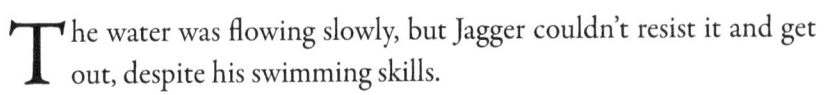

---

The water was flowing slowly, but Jagger couldn't resist it and get out, despite his swimming skills.

With lightning speed, Eleanor ran back to inform everyone. They quickly gathered along the river, searching frantically for him, but to no avail.

---

"YOU, you're the one who killed him, all because of you!" Jagger's father screamed at Eleanor, his face contorted with rage.

---

With disdain and anger, everyone looked at her, this peculiar child. She fled to her home and sought refuge in her father's arms, crying. "It's not my fault, it's not my fault," she repeated amidst her father's bewildered gaze, unaware of the situation, gazed at her with concern.

After she explained what happened, he said, 'Don't worry, my dear. I've got this. I'll go take care of it.' He gave her a reassuring nod, then turned and walked briskly towards Jagger's house...

---

He returned an hour later and reassured her: "He's okay, my dear. They found him." Those two words eased and lifted a heavy weight off Eleanor's burdened heart.

---

However, at Jagger's doorstep, his father, sitting in the car, said sternly, "I don't want to see your face. This is all because of your negligence. Take her to the mental hospital."

She tossed the mask with resentment and eventually fell asleep after a long bout of crying. Meanwhile, her parents remained clueless about what to do!

Even at school, she could hear the bullies' voices: "She's the one who killed him, it's her, I saw her!" Her classmates used to repeat these phrases.

The once grand estate of the Jagger family now stood silent and forlorn. The luxury cars were gone, replaced by a thick layer of dust on the driveway. Weeds began to creep into the manicured gardens, reclaiming the space with wild abandon. The windows, once gleaming, were now dull and lifeless, reflecting the emptiness within.

Eleanor often found herself walking past the house, her steps slowing as she approached. She would pause at the gate, her eyes tracing the familiar path to the front door. Memories of laughter and shared secrets echoed in her mind, now replaced by an eerie silence. The house seemed to watch her, its empty windows like eyes filled with accusation and sorrow.

One day, she noticed a broken swing in the backyard, swaying gently in the breeze. It was the same swing where she and Jagger had spent countless afternoons, their laughter mingling with the rustling leaves. Now, it creaked with a haunting rhythm, a ghostly reminder of what once was.

Eleanor's heart ached with a mix of guilt and nostalgia; the house, abandoned and decaying, mirrored her own sense of loss and isolation. Each time she passed by, she felt a pang of longing for the days when the house was alive with warmth and friendship.

"I've told you before, even if the idea lingered in my head, I managed to tame it after all these years. Yes, it's been 12 years," Eleanor said, her voice steady but tinged with the weight of the past.

She turned to Henry, who was dozing off beside her. "What about you, Henry? Wake up," she said, shaking his shoulder gently.

Henry stirred, blinking sleepily. "Sorry, Elly. I must have drifted off," he mumbled, rubbing his eyes. "What were you saying?"

Eleanor smiled softly, the corners of her eyes crinkling. "Just reminiscing about old times. It's been a long journey, hasn't it?"

Henry nodded, fully awake now. "Yeah, it has. But look at how far you've come. You're stronger than you think."

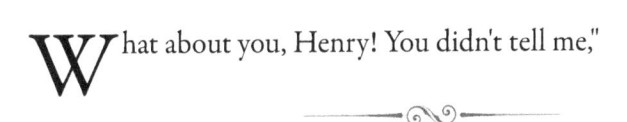

---

What about you, Henry! You didn't tell me,"

---

Oh, mine! That sounds like quite an ordeal. Mine wasn't as disastrous as yours. When I was about six years old, my father brought me a couple of rabbits to breed. After four months passed with no baby rabbits, he decided to slaughter them with his friend. I prepared the wood and lit the fire. His two friends were afraid, so he took the knife, and oops, everything was finished. Their souls came inside mine," Henry shared, his voice tinged with a mix of sadness and resignation.

"Oh, poor rabbits!" Eleanor expressed her regret, her eyes softening with empathy. "That must have been tough, Henry. It's strange how these moments from our childhood stay with us, shaping who we become."

Henry nodded, a small smile playing on his lips. "Yeah, they do. But we learn to carry them, don't we?"

---

"What truly matters now is that I have found you. I'll replace your sorrows with happiness. Believe me," He added, his voice filled with sincerity.

Eleanor looked at him, her heart warming at his words. "Thank you, Henry. That means a lot to me."

---

...

---

On the other side, Jessica and the girls were in the forum. Meanwhile, Lori and Sophie returned to the center in Belgravia.

Jessica exhaled deeply before saying, "Thank God, she finally left. We got rid of her,"

Lily said, her voice dripped with jealousy. "This bitch, if I had her beauty, I'd rule the world."

"Hah! Her beauty! You might need glasses," Jessica retorted.

Elsie chimed in, defending the unseen beauty, "Come on, Jessica, you know she's gorgeous."

Jessica scoffed, «Only guys know who the gorgeous one is" she declared confidently. With a decisive wink, she exited the forum.

The others hesitated for a moment but inevitably followed her lead. Each claimed beauty for themselves alone...

"Thank goodness everything's alright. I hope it doesn't happen again," sighed Lori as she settled into her office.

# Chapter 6

Sunday, May, 28th 2024 the final trophy of a Stableford match play competition.

It was sunny day, perfect weather, and an enthusiastic atmosphere with a large crowd. Spectators moved between the holes along the course to follow the players and enjoy the intense competition and impressive performances. While others had a different opinion about the final, something else brought them here. They came for a different kind of competition.

"Who gets the wealthiest guy, and who wins the most beautiful woman."

In the main stands, Lori and Sophie were seated side by side. The gleam of their glasses sparkles in the light of their golden hair, emitting flashes like rays of the sun with every swing they take. They vary the conversation topics from time to time.

While Jessica and Lilly left the forum after taking their adornment. Jessica wore a tight bleu short jean, while Lilly was wearing a back golf skirt with white t-shirt. This revealing attire stood as a witness to their intentions in this final.

Lori asked, "Who do you think is responsible for these insolences?"

Sophie replied with a jealous tone, "Who else could it be but Eleanor! She's here every day."

Lorie: "No way, I know her inside out. She's not interested in relationships like that."

Sophie insisted: "Don't forget, she's the forum manager."

"However, I'm sure it's not her."
"When the managers fails, they must resign or be dismissed."
"Please enough, Sophie. I've told you it's not her."

After engaging in verbal exchanges and debates, Lori left the golf course, heading toward the car harbor. There, she was met with a shocking sight: all the tires of her car had been deliberately slashed with a knife. It was at this moment that she began to sense the gravity of the situation.

Rather than attending the competition, Eleanor found herself at Henry's apartment, seated before his laptop as Henry gradually scrolled through the images of an island, which had been acquired by a new billionaire and some investors, begun with the azure, translucent waters caressing the white sandy beaches, surrounded by majestic palms and bent mango trees. It then leads us into the heart of the dense, untamed forest, with its virgin flowers that have never been touched by human or jinn hands.

These blooms unfurl their vibrant colors under the melodies of the soaring birds. Nestled far away from the clamor of the contemporary world, there lies a quaint city, a realm of dreams. It is akin to a concealed cocoon, shielding within it bodies that have long been deemed peculiar by the masses.

These bodies are guarded by its nacre, until they transform into pearls, unlike any other found in our world.

With a capacity to accommodate over 10,000 visitors annually, and rooms designated for each category, even underground chambers, North Island ...awaiting official documents to change its name, has declared itself as a unique island on planet Earth.

"It's not just an island, Ellie, it's our new home." Henry said, pointing to the pictures.

"You can take all the therians you know." He added.

"I can't believe my eyes! Who's that lion"

"He's the island clown, the hope bringer. And this is his assistant the fox" Henry answered.

With great enthusiasm, Eleanor began forming a mental list. It wasn't long, but she wanted to help all the therians who were struggling like her.

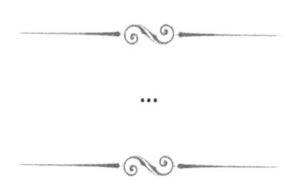

...

In the early morning of the next Saturday, Eleanor's footsteps were heavy as she approached Lori's porch. With cup of coffee held in one hand and a book in the other. Lori's expression was one of astonishment as she glanced up from her reading to see Eleanor standing there.

"Eleanor, you scared me! What's up?"

Lori asked, setting down her coffee cup.

Eleanor took a deep breath. "Hey, good morning, I wanted to tell you that I'm leaving the group. I can't keep up anymore."

Lori's brow furrowed. "What! What's wrong? Is there something bothering you?"

"No, no," Eleanor said, shaking her head. "I'm leaving England tomorrow... I think I've found my purpose."

Eleanor met Lori's gaze, a newfound determination in her eyes. "I've been doing a lot of thinking, and I realized that my heart lies elsewhere. There's something I need to do, something I feel called to pursue. It's not an easy decision, but it's the right one for me."

Lori studied her friend's face, seeing the conviction there. "Well, if you've given it this much thought, then I trust you. But I'm going to miss you, Eleanor. You've been such an important part of our society."

"I'm going to miss all of you too. But I'm following my heart"

Lori nodded slowly, a bittersweet smile tugging at her lips. "Then I wish you all the best, Eleanor. I hope you find what you're looking for."

Eleanor returned the smile, her eyes twinkling with a mixture of excitement and trepidation. "Thank you Lori for all you've done to me. This isn't goodbye forever, I promise. I'll be back someday."

"Are you really leaving that fast?"

"The homeland calls. I can't explain it to you." And she threw herself into Lori's embrace; that chest which had always embraced her and stood by her during the toughest times of her career.

It was a moment of parting where hearts break, and perhaps it is easier for Eleanor this time, as she had the chance to embrace and stay close. Unlike Jagger, who only received a gesture and a distant glance.

---

...

## 106 Harpesford Avenue England 08:00 Pm

As the Bentley Mulsanne Grand Limousine comes to a halt, the chauffeur steps out in his formal attire and open the door with his pristine white gloves, saying, "Please, ladies, step inside."

With exchanged looks of astonishment, Jessica and Lily climb aboard, both disbelieving what they are witnessing with their own eyes.

"Are you ready, ladies? Pablo jests. And the chauffeur headed to Farnborough Airport.

The limousine's elegance glided through the tranquil road amidst the beauty of the countryside, where the runways and lined-up aircraft stood as a gateway to a world of luxury.

"Hello sir, we are at your disposal for departure." The flight attendant, stated politely.

"Welcome aboard the Sky gem. We extend a warm welcome and wish you a pleasant and comfortable journey to St Tropez. Please don't hesitate to contact any of the crew members if you need assistance or have any special requests. We look forward to serving you during this flight." The pilot announced.

---

...

---

The Pagana Huayra's wing doors spread open like a soaring hawk in the sky, as Henry calls out to Eleanor: 'Are you longing for the journey?'

"Oh my God, where did you get this?' summarizes Eleanor's astonishment vividly and powerfully."

"I'll tell you on the way."

And the Pagana dashed off like a cheetah in the savannah; Lori couldn't believe her eyes at what she saw from the window overlooking the road.

"Who the hell is this?"

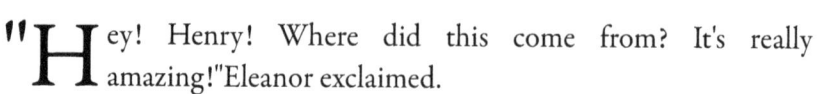

---

"Hey! Henry! Where did this come from? It's really amazing!"Eleanor exclaimed.

Henry: "Well, let's say I am a personal lifestyle manager for some wealthy individuals.

"Lifestyle manager! I haven't heard of it before."

---

My tasks are not general but are limited to providing luxury service and unique attention to each one of them, such as managing special requests... or... procuring rare and sometimes even weird items. Yeah, weird"

Eleanor's eyes fixed at Henry as she remembered something: "Can you handle my request also?"

Henry: "Absolutely, I'm your genie in the lamp"
Eleanor: "Take me to Chicago ink tattoo when we arrive."
Henry: "Ha-ha, that's it! Alright, considered it done!"

...

After two hours of flying, the Sky gem landed at La Mole Airport, Saint Tropez. There, they were picked up by a Mercedes AMG.

Pablo, in a commanding tone, instructed the chauffeur, "The girls have a desire for shopping. Take them to the finest swimwear boutique."

In the midst of the candy-colored buildings and the narrow streets that exude a special charm, promise elegance and a unique experience, Jessica and Lily are still in a state of shock, a shock that surpasses their dreams and expectations.

The mesmerising journey had transported them from one world to another. How could the world be so beautiful? How did the distances shrink and become close, even comfortable to an indescribable degree, as if the earth folded and shortened its distances? The sunny yellows, sky blues, and mint greens - colors filling their hearts with pure happiness, smiles, and a sense of joy!

Even better, shopping at elegant French designer boutiques is like discovering a treasure trove of luxurious fashion and innovative craftsmanship. Truly, this elegance is unlike any other.

Lily held up the delicate G-string bikini, the shimmering white fabric catching the sunlight that streamed through the open window. Her eyes shone with excitement as she turned to her friend Jessica. "What do you think of this?" she asked, eagerness apparent in her voice.

Jessica smiled "It's stunning" "The white really suits your skin tone beautifully." She paused, then held up her own selection - black tropical bikini adorned with colourful flowers, embodying the spirit of the city they now called home.

They meandered between the shops, sometimes making purchases and other times strolling, their hands occasionally intertwining against each other until they reached the car.

Pablo made a few sniffs then said: "aw, you smell good!"

Jessica replied, "Yeah, it's the famous classique édition summer, it kills me"

"Let me smell it" Pablo requested. Mm you're nasty Jessica. He chuckled.

"I bought Spirituous Double Vanilla," Lily said as she sprayed some on Pablo.

"You are naughty girls," he said flirtatiously to them.

"You haven't seen Jessica's bikini yet." Lily's voice said in an intimate tone.

Jessica wondered, "Are we going to your place?"

"Oh my God, how beautiful the air caresses these perfumes." let me enjoy these moments"

"I am just asking"

Pablo raises an eyebrow in a sarcastic tone and says, "Actually, it's my father's house." Then he follows up with a light laugh.

While Lily, looking out the window, her heart is full of love for Pablo, and she whispered to the breeze, «Maybe he loves Jessica."

With the soft vibrations of the car, and the warmth of the perfume, Jessica and Lily's ears aroused and blood rushed to their cheeks, until their nerves were tense.

Extreme actions or emotions can lead to their opposites, If reaches their maximum. Like snow, which seems gentle, can cause harm if handled excessively, and laughter, when taken to the extreme, can indeed become exhausting or even deadly.

And here is the last turn, where the driver parks the car at the end of 1 Chem. des Amoureux, and once he drops them off, he says goodbye and sets off again.

"Is this the house?" Lily asked, her eyes staring at the two-story building, and the ordinary shops beneath it."

«Still forward, why the rush?» Pablo replied

Immediately after they crossed the road, the alley flanked by neatly parked cars, and the orderly rows led them to the port side, where the Sea Gem was moored quietly beside the wharf like a gorgeous gold ingot shimmering among the rusty iron pieces, waiting for her dream knight to rescue her from the worn surrounding.

...

Unlike Jessica and Lily's journey, Eleanor's was somewhat challenging due to the distance. However, Henry fulfilled his promise in just ten hours and booked her an appointment with one of the most renowned artists in Chicago Ink tattoo."

The artist says, "Do you have a specific design in mind, or would you prefer we start from scratch?"

"Yes, it's already in my head"

"Great, let's start with the description, and then we'll discuss any improvement or modification before we proceed." The artist's pen and paper ready to bring life to her vision.

"It's a cheetah fur; I want it to cover my entire back and...Make it looks as realistic as possible."

"Amazing! The design will look fantastic on your back. We'll focus on intricate details to make it as realistic as possible. Do you have any preferences regarding colors or patterns?"

"Absolutely, that's a crucial aspect. I want a vibrant spotted pattern, and the colors should be more animalistic and vivid."

After a few minutes, the artist presented the preliminary design to her.

"I'm excited to turn your vision into reality."

With high skill and great dedication, the artist's needle began planting the cheetah fur on Eleanor's back, and lo and behold, it gradually started to come to life.

---

...

---

The Sea gem crew welcomed the owner, lined up in opposing rows of five, all adorned, facing each other in opposite rows, with five on each side.

Meanwhile, Pablo and the girls walked in the middle until they reached the main hall.

"Okay, for anyone who wants to shower, here's the shower," Pablo said, pointing with his finger to the corner of the spacious hall.

"Oh, it's wonderful!" Lily responded with joy and delight.

With only a few pieces of furniture, semi-circular couches encircled the small gray tables, all surrounded by glass windows from every direction, showcasing the opulence and exclusivity of the design in every aspect.

"In fact, my father owns five yachts, but we rarely use them, they're rented out throughout the year."

"Five? Wow!" Lily amazed; her mouth wide open in astonishment!

"Pablo, you always surprise us with your 'unexpected' outings," Jessica said, feeling a throbbing between her legs.

"I think I need a drink to calm my nerves. Where's the fridge, Pablo?"

Pablo, admiring their beauty mixed with naivety, replied, "There is no fridge here, my dear. This is a very private suite." He walked towards the telephone hanging on the wall and said, "Send the food and drinks."

As they talked for a short while, the dining table appeared from an opening in the floor delivered via the elevator.

The girls didn't stop asking Pablo about the names of the various and rare dishes.

"You can ask the chef later," Pablo replied to them. Now, I think your swimsuits have missed you?"

"Impossible, you want us to drown after all this food?" Lily, with a voice filled with fullness from the food, and her hand on her stomach."

"Follow me up when you're ready"

He said, as he hurried up the stairs.

The girls followed him immediately, and as soon as Lily stepped onto the last step, she exclaimed, "Oh my God!" Then she turned to Jessica, "I think I've changed my mind," before heading towards her bag to look for her G string. As Jessica tries to steal a glance towards the upper deck, uncovered, and covered with Lily's body.

On the edge of the finely crafted crystal frame, Pablo, handsomely rugged, lounges relaxed inside the Jacuzzi; his chest muscles bulging outward with a hint of fuzz in the center, glistening with bronzing oil. Through his sunglasses, the undulating White Sea waves were gently reflected, as his hand adorned with a large diamond watch reached for the Salvatore's Legacy glass.

As Pablo takes another sip of the rich, velvety wine, the gorgeous brunette Jessica appeared. The sunlight reflects on her emerald eyes, pear body and curvaceous beauty, which instantly captivates his heart. She saunters over to the Jacuzzi, her hips swaying with a seductive grace to join him, especially the view of tropical bikini absorbed by her body.

Pablo's eyes are immediately captivated to her, fixed as they scan the elegant curves of her body while she approaches, and drawn to the confidence and sensuality on the way she moves.

With a coy smile on her face, she pauses. Then, she slowly descends into the warm, bubbling water, ensuring ample opportunity for admiration of her alluring, swelled breasts and the breadth of her arse. The water glistens on her skin, accentuating her natural beauty and heightening the sensual atmosphere.

Pablo plunges with her; quickly their movements become more deliberate, their laughter tinged with subtle hints of seduction. Each leans closer to the other, until her breast touches his arms; a sign of love, expanding in the tightness, and contracting in the wild.

"Pablo, your eyes look simply Devin." Jessica purrs, maintaining eye contact, sparkling with mischief."

"He stares into her right eye, then utters." Like yours"

"Suddenly, the sound of a plunge erupts, disturbing the water."You sneaky traitors, why didn't you wait for me?"Lily grins.

"Pablo dives underwater and lifts Lily onto the sky, then throws her again on the big Jacuzzi, while she screams with joy, her golden hair glowing in the air with a halo of radiance."

"The interplay of childish bickering and sensual flirting throughout the evening created an atmosphere dominated by comfort, security, and intimacy.

"Now it's time for fun," Pablo announced, "follow me."

Everyone, head down to the lower deck, at the rear of the yacht where the black jet skis are parked, Pablo directed, swiftly tossing one into the sea, and he started helping them down.

Lily sat in the front, almost reclining between his thighs, while Jessica sat behind, her hands wrapped around his chest.

"Hold on tight, "Let's set sail!"

The Yamaha set off along the coast until they reached the beach overlooking the city of Nice. Pablo asked Lily to hold the wheel, while he held her soft waist with his right hand and whispered in her ear: 'Hold it tight, you have to feel it! ... Don't let it slip away from you... You're amazing!' The warm breeze made Lily sigh from the tickle every time he whispered in her ear. His left hand was holding Jessica's hand, occasionally turning to her, so their cheeks met.

Jessica playfully nibbles on the peaks of Pablo's chest between her fingers, while other hand slowly ventures southward, nearly reaching the waistband; the same thing as Pablo's action to Lily. The mixture of fear, excitement, and arousal in the silent sea, turned on the guys without saying a word. And what add fuel to fire, was Jessica taking off the top bikini, and sticking her heart on Pablo's back, which led to a juicy kiss between them, and Lily's statement with warm and intimacy "Please, shall we return...

---

...

Hampstead Heath, London
Following Eleanor's departure, Lori's circumstances began to deteriorate progressively. The threats against her escalated, and her sense of personal safety dwindled. Despite lodging numerous complaints with the authorities and being provided with round-the-clock security, the menacing messages continued unabated. It became increasingly clear to her that the situation was far more perilous than she had initially imagined. This criminal syndicate had not only outstripped the reach of local law enforcement but had also established a formidable international presence.

All this was the result of her stubbornness and refusal to follow the gang's plan, which aimed to topple major political figures and even heads of state by luring them into illicit activities at the forum, secretly recording them, and using the footage to exert pressure on them in the future.

Each time she filed a lawsuit against those who ordered her to comply; she was met with even greater threats than before. Death threats reached her despite the tight security around her. It became clear to her that she was no match for them. The situation was far more formidable than she had ever imagined.

"Twin twin," A message chimed on Lori's phone.

Eleanor's entirely tattooed back met Lori's eyes as soon as she opened the message. Leaving her dumbfounded as she scrutinized the details of the tattoo, mesmerized by it and other times puzzled about the reason drove Eleanor to this.

With eyes full of perplexity, Lori wondered to herself: "Eleanor has gone mad! What should I reply to her?"

She typed a few letters but soon deleted them, afraid of bullying Eleanor, before ending up crafting a reply: 'Wow, that's intense ❤'

"It seems like you're realizing the American dream!"

"Not the American dream, but freedom."

Then, Lori made a video call. For the first time, she cried in front of Eleanor.

"Help me, Eleanor," Lori said the fear evident on her face.

Eleanor's expression turned serious, her concern growing. "Lori, what's happened? Why are you so scared?"

"They're threatening me, Eleanor. It's getting worse every day. I don't know what to do anymore," Lori replied, her voice trembling.

"Who is threatening you? What do they want?" Eleanor asked, leaning closer to the screen.

"It's the gang. They want me to carry out their orders, and when I refuse, they escalate the threats. I don't think I can handle this on my own anymore," Lori confessed, wiping away her tears.

"I'll be back soon. I won't leave you alone," Eleanor assured her, her voice firm with determination.

---

"No need to come back, Eleanor. You're safe there," Lori said, her voice still shaky.

Eleanor shook her head. "I can't just stay here knowing you're in danger. We'll figure this out together."

"But I don't want you to risk your safety for me," Lori insisted.

"Lori, you mean too much to me. I won't stand by and do nothing," Eleanor replied firmly. "We'll find a way to put an end to this, I promise."

"Stay safe, Lori. I'll handle this," Eleanor said before ending the call, her mind already racing with plans to help her friend.

---

...

---

Jessica went upstairs first followed by Lily, then both headed to the shower in the upper deck's corner. Meanwhile Pablo left the Yamaha for the two crew members to pull up‘ and he took a light inspection tour inside his paradise, which had almost been organized.

The cozy plush sofas by the Jacuzzi side were inviting, offering comfortable seating amidst the shared colors of the wrapped bath towels, pillows, and the coffee set placed on striped placemats of the low tables. This harmony served as a testament to the outstanding and thoughtful design, letting no choice for Jessica and Lily but to jump in.

They flipped over hunting the sun ray, like it's the last summer's day. The sun's kisses on Lily's blond rear almost nude flushed it into a rosy hue, setting a sultry scene for Pablo's arrival.

Suddenly, Pablo leaped between them, after, exclaimed" You mischief makers, where is my place?"

Jessica gasped, 'Oh my God!" And Lily's body tensed up, nearly slipped on the wet deck in shock," Wow, You fool, you startled me!" Then laughter filled the air, immediately after the fear subsided..."

"My heart is beating fast, touch it," Lily said, asking Jessica to feel her pulse.

Jessica placed her palm hand on Lily's chest, then moved it slightly beneath her breast, and said, 'It's really fast.'"

Lily looked into Jessica's enchanting emerald eyes, unable to control her desire, with a light sigh almost inaudible followed by, "Look how petit they are."

Jessica replied " yeah, they are, and silky" while she made a subtle squeeze with her thumb, her unwavering gaze fixed upon the right azure eye of Lily, coupled with the tantalizing gesture of biting her lips, all conveyed an unmistakable expression of interest in her.

This had never crossed their minds before, but gazing into the right eye harbored its own secret, serving as one of the pathways to heart's entwine and love souls.

However, Pablo had something else to say. He uttered, reclining among them. "I see you falling in love!"

The girls responded modestly, and Lily chuckled, 'I don't know what's happening, I can't express this feeling!'"

Meanwhile, the drunkenness hadn't left Jessica yet. Whereupon, she murmured intimately, 'She's enchanting.'

"Why don't we crown this love with what it deserves?" Pablo, flirtatiously Coaxed, the explicitness was presented in fondling their peaks.

"But how?" The girls purred, horniness evident on their faces eagerly anticipating sex.

Pablo whispered with desire, "The naughty bits are a passage to the souls."

In the meantime, Jessica nibbled on Lily's lips, as they made out passionately, the kisses fervently wrestling each other, and their moans loudly echoed across the deck...

"Your mouth is warm, I like it" Lily said.

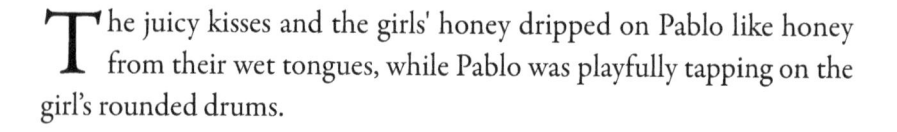

---

The juicy kisses and the girls' honey dripped on Pablo like honey from their wet tongues, while Pablo was playfully tapping on the girl's rounded drums.

---

There was an everyday threesome until the weekend. Even though it wasn't planned beforehand, silly Pablo, as the girls claimed, had properly arranged everything in advance.

Before the last night of departure, the walkie talkie's beep buzzing static disturbed the infatuated trio, immersed in their desires.

The head of the crew came through the walkie-talkie, 'Mr. Pablo, I wish to inform you that you have received a special invitation, over."

"Copy that. Who sent it? Out"

"It's from the officials of the Cannes Festival, over."

With The last word uttered, Jessica and Lily pull their tongues away from the shared ice cream between their lips, and with raised eyebrows, they exchanged a curious glance filled with wonder.

# Chapter 7

## THE QUEEN'S WEDDING

The following day, the phone sounded, and the same individual's voice stated, "The wedding is scheduled for next month, I do not wish for any unexpected occurrences."

"Acknowledged, I will handle it."

---

Eleanor spent a week in Chicago, unimpressed by the magnificence of the Peninsula Hotel, after Henry had left her there. Her blue eyes would flash a gleam whenever she passed through the hotel lobby, and they would receive the subtle hints of flirting from passersby. Their luminance reflected a longing for the new homeland, while everyone else made assumptions about her. Now he is returning once more, to take her on one final journey, to The North Island, Seychelles.

"I must return to England immediately, Henry," Eleanor said.

"Impossible. What's wrong, Eleanor?" Henry replied, his brows furrowing with concern.

After she explained the situation to him, he promised to take charge and solve the problem as soon as they reached the island. However, there was no turning back now.

On the other side, The Crimson Ship didn't sail without a leader. After Eleanor's resignation, Lori soon declared Sophie as the new manager and overseer, hoping she would set things right there, as Sophie was vehemently opposed to this sort of submission to men. However, events quickly turned upside down this time, as maternal instinct took the upper hand. This innate instinct within every woman persists and remains, even if she tries to deny it.

"Hello ma'am, it seems you're new here. I haven't seen you before!"

"I am the new head of the forum, Sophie."

"Nice to meet you Sophie, I'm Mr. Wellington."

"Oh hello, nice to meet you too."

"If you need anything, don't hesitate to let me know, miss." He bid her farewell with a kiss on her hand, and then departed.

His neat appearance and good manners reflected his high status in English society, but Sophie did not know who he was yet until she entered the forum.

"Do you know Mr. Wellington, whom I just met?" she asked the cleaning staff.

"Ah, Mr. Wellington, the gentleman, yes, I don't know much about him but I believe he is from an aristocratic family."

And Sophie awakened from her slumber and reassessed herself. The dignity of Mr. Wellington and his gentle personality made her wish she had a son like him. She often imagined what it would be like to raise a boy with his charm and kindness, envisioning the joy and pride such a child would bring into her life.

---

In Saint-Tropez, the girls were visibly anxious before the big day. Choosing their party outfits was their sole preoccupation, after Pablo had agreed to bring the two fruits with him to the Cannes Film Festival party. The girls left no upscale boutique unvisited and no dress untried, until they finally settled on two chic gowns from a lesser-known French label, rather than the more famous ones.

"Let's seek Pablo's opinion, as he has the expertise," Jessica suggested, then Lily called out, "Pablo, can you come down for a moment please!"

""I am busy, you can come up," Pablo shouted from the deck.

With elegance and confidence, they began to present themselves to Pablo. Lily was first, in her long white dress with a slit up to her knee, embodying the elegance of simplicity. She was followed by Jessica, in a form-fitting dress that hugged her curvaceous figure, the vibrant red color captivating the eye. Its title was 'Gorgeous'.

With gentle applause and a glance from behind his glasses, Pablo responded, saying: "Wonderful, superb."

"Come on, Pablo, don't jest, and tell me the truth." Lily insisted.

"Absolutely, you all look fantastic."

After applying the final touches to everyone's makeup, Pablo glanced at his watch and said urgently: 'I'm in the car, don't be late. It's only a play, not your wedding.' He then hurried off to join the driver.

After a quarter of an hour and several calls from Pablo, the girls joined him.

Finally the years of patient anticipation melted away, Eleanor's plane touched down at the Therians airport situated on the mountain meadow. Here, on this island shrouded in mystery and intrigue, the only mode of transportation available was the majestic giant elephants - yes, elephants fused with the bodies of humans - ready to take you wherever your heart desires.

"Good morning, sir. Where might you be headed?" inquired the elephant, his voice laced with a hint of intrigue and curiosity.

"Good morning!" replied Eleanor, her gaze flickering with a hint of uncertainty and wonder, as it landed on Henry.

"Please, take us to the city," implored Henry, his tone tinged with a heady mix of urgency and excitement.

With a fluid grace, the therians lifted Eleanor onto his shoulders, and in that moment, a world of luxurious decadence and enigmatic allure opened up before their very eyes. It was a world where the finest things in life were merged with the alluring mystery of the unknown, suffused with a touch of bittersweet melancholy.

As they set out on their ride, Eleanor and Henry could feel the elephant's powerful muscles rippling beneath them, propelling them forward with an effortless grace. It was a sensation that hinted at a world beyond the mundane, a realm where the airport and the city were separated by a dense forest of varied-sized trees. A winding mountain road cut through it, adding to its enigmatic allure. As they journeyed for about three miles, the city emerged from beneath the trees, its grand waterfall cascading down onto the vast lake, leaving Eleanor humbled and awed by the breathtaking view.

"Cheers, here you go," said Henry before paying him for the ride.

With moderate steps, Henry and Eleanor entered the city, where tranquility prevailed, and its streets were semi-deserted. This piqued Eleanor's curiosity.

"Where are the residents?" she inquired.

"I'm not sure, let keep walking." And as they approached the lake, they spotted a man sitting on his wooden chair, sometimes gazing at the cascading waterfall pouring onto the lake and other times adding a touch to his artistic painting, which he could hardly finish, until Henry surprised him. "My friend Alfred, how are you?"

The man turned around, the owl mask covering his entire head. "Henry, it's been too long! Come here, friend," said Alfred cheerfully.

After they had embraced in greeting, Henry inquired of the others. Alfred informed him, declaring:

"They're at the racetrack; today is the first horse racing competition on the island. You should go join them, but after you tell me about the new arrival..."

Eleanor replied, "Oh, sorry, I'm Eleanor, Henry's friend."

"Welcome to your home." Alfred said warmly to Eleanor.

"Thank you very much, Alfred, that's very kind of you."

As soon as they entered the racetrack, Eleanor was surprised to see the stands packed with spectators of all kinds, and the Therian horses raced swiftly, each with a number on its back.

Eleanor quickly embraced the cheers of the crowd, sending her encouragement with loud shouts, as if she had previously bet on one of the participating horses. Her excessive enthusiasm led her to be noticed by a tigress in the highest stands, especially when she saw some tattoos on Eleanor's shoulders, indicating hostile intentions.

However, Henry was by her side to protect her, as the law of the island also stipulates that any assault or bullying will lead to the perpetrator's expulsion from the island, so the tigress recoiled.

Those blissful moments of celebration and warm embrace from the crowds on the first day, swept away all the strange fears and doubts of the newcomer, who quickly blended in with this kind community, as though she had been a resident of this land since time immemorial.

The race has come to an end, and the spectators started leaving one after the other, each heading in their own direction. Among them were Rebecca pulling her dog Felix, and Evelyn following to her right the playful cat Katie on tow, and other people strolled by, each with their faithful therian companion at their side, who had chosen to live alongside humans, becoming a normal part of daily existence for the people they had bonded with.

---

Cannes, Théâtre de la Croisette.
Had it not been for the exclusivity of the invitation and the elegance of the attire, the guests would have walked; instead, they chose to drive. Shortly after, winding through charming alleys, past luxurious hotels and glass-fronted shops, they found themselves before the stately Théâtre de la Croisette, standing proudly beside Le Palais des Festivals.

"Where shall we sit?" said Lilly, her eyes sweeping over the red velvet chairs and the elegant design that harmonized authenticity with sophistication.

"Let's go upstairs," suggested Pablo.

"Let me, I'm afraid of heights," said Jessica, then they settled into a seat in the third row, while the rest of the seats were almost entirely empty, "I think we arrived a bit early!" Pablo remarked.

"Don't fret, we're on time; others will come," Jessica replied, ardently in her eyes, and indeed, the invitees began arriving one by one, with whispers here and laughter there. Gradually, the vibrant red of the chairs faded away, replaced by a spectrum of clothing colors - sometimes modest, sometimes daring.

Among the notable attendees was director Edward Lasberg, the mischievous young man whose reputation quickly rose due to his captivating and controversial advertisements. He was sitting in the seat right of the first-floor staircase, and backstage corridor, with his lover Kotryna, who never left him wherever he went, until he grew tired of her.

While his second lover Sadie, the event coordinator, was alternating between the stage and behind the curtain to ensure that things were running smoothly.

Her hands trembled slightly as she adjusted her earpiece for the umpteenth time, eyes darting between the stage setup and the backstage chaos. Until she passed by them, her brow furrowed in deep concentration from far, then she reached them with a forced smile stretched across her face, accompanied by a brief nod of acknowledgment, exchanging a polite greeting between them, before she continued on her way, "Good evening, and welcome" she murmured, the words strained yet cordial. Meanwhile he pretended not to know her, he feigned obliviousness, and his gaze fixed on the program schedule in his hands.

Things quickly became confusing for Edward as his thoughts jumbled together, his eyes filled with uncertainty. "Good heavens, is this possible?" he wondered silently when his eyes fell upon the third lover, whom he had only met two weeks ago, talking to Sadie, her cousin. And who completely ignored him when she saw Kotryna laughing heartily at the impact of his short jokes and her arm intertwined with his.

The curtain rose, unveiling the characters and marking the start of the play, with applause, laughter, and tears, as is customary in theatrical pieces.

Handheld fans danced left and right in the hands of the women. As everyone's gaze was focused intently on the stage, Edward sensually bit his lip; the beads of glistening sweat mixed with Lily's light makeup captivated his mind. He couldn't tear his eyes away from her for even a moment, disregarding his current lover, who was present in body but absent in mind, absorbed in the events of the theatrical plot.

As the first scene of the play passed, then the second, every glance Edward directed towards Lily made his stomach and liver tremble. That feeling, the childhood passion he had long forgotten, he now felt it again. Overpowered by desire this time, he forgot about the three altogether, and began his journey of observation, aiming to pick up her.

Lily didn't pay attention to his flirtatious hints, on the contrary, she responded with shy smiles that stirred his intestines more and stirred his innermost feelings.

While cooling herself slowly with the fan's breeze, she accidentally turned it on the back side and placed it below her mouth.

Edward, well-versed in women's wiles, immediately understood the signal—the discreet invitation—and gestured discreetly in response, 'Meet me outside.' With a subtle nod of his head, unnoticed by anyone but them, he asked her to follow him into the backstage corridor. Lily looked right and left, raised her eyebrows in uncertainty, and placed a finger on her chest.

"Me..."

Edward took a cigarette from the packet and sighed, "I'll be back soon." He murmured to his partner and headed inside the corridor. Lily hesitated for a moment, and then followed him inside the corridor, unnoticed by Jessica, who was resting her head on Pablo's chest.

"Finally, we managed to escape. Phew," Edward said with a smile.

Lily looked around cautiously and responded, "Aw, is this an escape?"

"I'm Edward, the casting director." He introduced himself.

Lily leaned against the wall, her lips pursed as if she was about to kiss. "Ah, so you want me to be your next movie star?"

Edward was surprised by the response, but he quickly went along with it and said, "And who else would be the star?"

Lily flashed a teasing smile, stepping closer. "Tell me when you're ready for my performance." she teased back, her voice dropping slightly lower, adding a hint of allure to her words.

Edward chuckled again, enjoying the banter. "I'm always ready," he replied smoothly, meeting her gaze with equal intensity. "But keep it secret, so the other star doesn't find out."

Lily poked her head out from the corridor and said, "Ah, the superstar, I can see her, she's beautiful" hinting to Kotryna.

Edward glanced around to ensure they were alone, then leaned in closer to Lily. "Yeah, But she doesn't have what the camera loves."

Lily's eyes sparkled with a mix of excitement and curiosity. "Oh really? And what exactly does the camera love?"

Edward's smile widened. "I can spot the stars from the first sight. Your smile, eyes, lips, you have the kind of presence that can't be taught. It's either there or it isn't."

Lily bit her lower lip, feigning modesty. "You're quite the flatterer, aren't you? But words are easy. Show me you're serious."

Edward's expression grew more intense. "Consider it done. I'll arrange a screen test for you. But remember, this has to stay between us. No one else can know, especially her."

Lily's smile was radiant. She whispered in his ear, "Don't let me down, Edward. I won't let you down."

Lily didn't let the chance slip by, recalling everything Pablo had said before. She arranged a meeting with Edward, seeing it as the path to her dreams. As she returned to her seat, her mind was already racing with astonishment and possibilities. Immediately upon sitting down, she surprised Jessica with a passionate kiss on the lips, leaving her and Pablo laughing in surprise.

Here's the white thread tears the black revealing the white of the sand and dangling palm leaves along the island's shore, heralding the dawn of a new Thursday, full of excitement as always had been here.

The last howls of wolves echo through the forested mountains as they leave to their hiding places among the rocks. Letting the morning therians woo for new wishes, except for today only, today belongs to the king beloved by the masses on this magical land.

"Today is the king's wedding day. At 5pm everyone goes to the beach, and everyone is invited, without exception."

The rooster crowed repeatedly in the middle of the city street.

Everybody's eyes sparkled with a hint of mischief behind their delicate, feathered masks and sophisticated appearance, while heading to the pristine beach where event will take place.

As they wove their way through the crowd, Eleanor felt a tingle of excitement and curiosity. What secrets did this island and its inhabitants hold? And what had brought her and Henry, with all their unresolved history, to this lavish celebration?

"It's quite a spectacle, isn't it?" Eleanor murmured, her voice low and sultry, as she leaned in close to Henry's ear. She could feel the warmth of his breath on her neck, and the familiar scent of his cologne sent a shiver down her spine.

Henry's jaw tightened, and for a moment, Eleanor thought she saw a flash of vulnerability in his eyes. "It is," he replied, his voice barely above a whisper. "Though I can't help but wonder what lies beneath the surface of all this... opulence."

Eleanor nodded, her gaze sweeping across the crowd. "Precisely, there's something about this place that feels... _clandestine_."

"Actually, I've always been someone who opposes royal rule, but today, I don't know... I'm excited to see the Queen," Eleanor confessed to Henry, her voice tinged with a mix of surprise and anticipation.

"I've never witnessed grandeur like this!" exclaimed Henry, his eyes wide with wonder. "She truly is lucky, isn't she?" he added.

The guests began to arrive at the stunning white beach, surrounded by towering mountains, gathering at the area that had been prepared in advance with tables, draped in luxurious ivory linens, were adorned with elegant centrepieces of fresh flowers in vibrant colours. Crystal glasses and fine china gleamed in the soft light, while silver cutlery added a touch of sophistication.

Each table set under a spacious and airy tent, allowing the sea breeze to flow through freely. Each table featured intricate lace runners and beautifully crafted place cards, ensuring every detail exuded opulence and refinement. The Soft drapes and chandeliers hung from the ceilings, creating perfect havens for guests to relax and enjoy the moment.

Amidst the tables, a grand red rug path had been laid out for the king, leading directly to the central dais. The rich crimson of the rug stood in striking contrast to the soft, sandy beach, symbolising regal elegance and honouring the presence of royalty.

Above the central dais, a large poster proudly proclaimed, "Welcome to the north island" in bold, elegant lettering. The poster added a personal and festive touch to the event, greeting the guests and enhancing the island's unique charm.

After everyone had gathered and taken their seats, the peacock stood on the dais to deliver his speech:

"Dear Therians,

Welcome to your home! I'd like to thank each and every one of you for accepting our invitation. As you know, we were once scattered and struggled in this harsh world—some hidden away, others subjected to bullying, and tragically, many lost their lives. But today, thanks to our gracious king, we gather here in this homeland, breaking free from constraints and celebrating the freedom bestowed upon us by our king, Leopard."

At that moment, everyone stood in reverence and applauded "Leopard, Leopard," before the peacock raised his hand in the air to complete the speech. «However, it would be unjust to celebrate alone, and our King Leopard's joy has not yet been fulfilled. The king's crown gleam never shines without his queen and his dream, and a therian without a companion, is like a dark night without moonlight.

...And so, my fellow Therians, the queen is not just for the king himself, but for all of us to thrive, to love, and to be whole.

Before the peacock could finish what he was saying, and under the eager attention of the people, the king emerged from behind the curtains of the grand tent, wearing the leopard mask that concealed his face. His massive frame was adorned with vibrant tattoos that told tales of courage and heritage.

At that moment, every Therian paused, their hearts synchronising with each step he took towards them in a momentous occasion.

The sound of silence was audible in the shuffle of his bare feet, while the crowd wove a shared anticipation for the scene that had been etched in the annals of their history. As the king passed each table along the red carpet, a nod of the head expressed respect and esteem. His arrival was not merely a physical manifestation but a symbol of the unity and strength that had carried them to this day.

Finally, he stopped... and knelt on his knees before Henry's table, taking a ring box from his pocket. "Will you accept to be my queen, Eleanor?" he asked before removing the mask, his eyes gleaming with longing and tenderness.

Eleanor screamed, placing her hand over her mouth as tears streamed down her cheeks, unable to believe what she was seeing. She glanced at Henry, and then reached out to touch Jagger's cheeks with her hand. It was Jagger, her childhood companion, whom social classes had separated from her, yet he never forgot her for a moment.

"On that cursed day for Eleanor, when Jagger leapt into the river and was carried by the current towards the deep waters, Eleanor's first scream was enough to draw the attention of one of the fishermen standing on the riverbank, enjoying catching grayling. He saw the boy's life hanging by a thread as he struggled to survive in vain, with only a few meters left before reaching the rapidly flowing steep descent. But the noble man prevented the disaster with his swift intervention, acting just in time."

However, he entrusted Henry with the task of finding her and bringing her to him, regardless of the challenges involved and no matter what it took.

"Is all this for me?" she sighed through tears, addressing both Henry and Jagger together.

Jagger replied with a tone of regret mixed with hope, his hand on her cheek. "You deserve more, Eleanor. I'm sorry for what I've caused you." Then they embraced each other tightly, amidst the applause of the Therians and the calls of the peacock. "Long live Queen Eleanor, long live Queen Eleanor!" echoed the voices of all present.

And as Jagger embraced her on their way to the throne on the platform, a Therian hurriedly pulled away the covering of the previous sign, revealing the new one: "Eleanor's Island." Following him, the legal officer approached with a register and a pen, requesting Eleanor to sign the new name for the island...

Two years had passed since the mythical marriage, marking the greatest event in the kingdom's history. They declared complete independence from the nation it was formerly affiliated with, as King Jagger and his advisors solidified their self-rule over the island.

The anniversary of their union was celebrated with grandeur and solemnity, reflecting the deep respect and admiration the islanders held for their sovereign couple. Festivities adorned the streets, colorful banners swaying in the breeze, and the air redolent with the fragrance of exotic flowers from distant lands.

In the palace, Eleanor and Jagger stood side by side, their presence both commanding and approachable as they addressed nobles and commoners alike. They spoke not only of their triumphs but also of the challenges overcome in their second year together. Their words resonated not just as rulers but as partners united in a vision of prosperity and unity.

Under their stewardship, the island flourished. Economic reforms breathed new life into trade routes and agricultural practices, bringing prosperity even to the most remote corners of their domain. Educational initiatives empowered the youth, equipping them with knowledge and skills for a brighter future.

Politically, alliances were forged, and treaties signed, securing the island's autonomy and bolstering its position on the global stage. Islanders rallied behind their monarchs, proud of their sovereignty and resolute in defending it against any threat.

As the anniversary festivities drew to a close, Eleanor and Jagger shared a quiet moment on the palace balcony. They surveyed their kingdom bathed in the golden glow of the setting sun, overwhelmed with gratitude for the trust placed in them. Eleanor with a smiling gaze, watching her twins—a boy and a girl—playing in the garden. This scene was a perfect culmination of her love with Jagger.

In that serene moment, they realized their journey had only just begun. Challenges would inevitably arise, but with their love for each other and unwavering dedication to their people, they stood ready to navigate whatever the future held for their cherished island realm.

Henry returned to England, armed with a well-thought-out plan to save Lori. Their meeting gave rise to a thoughtful exchange on the issue at hand.

Every event that passed in Eleanor's life was shared openly with her friend and inspiration, Lori, through live video calls, where they exchanged joy and updates regularly.

Even news about Lily and Jessica reached Lori through TV channels and internet advertisements. Lily had achieved remarkable success as the main actress in a prestigious cosmetic company's television campaign. Through Lily's influence, Jessica also secured a role in an American TV series that earned her widespread popularity around the world.

But what shocked Lori the most and deeply affected her was the news of Sophie's wedding invitation with Mr. Wimbleton.

"At least she found someone to protect her, even if it's just a comforting embrace," she thought to herself.

This time, she felt a profound loneliness she had never expected to experience. All these images led her to find a new direction, a new purpose to discover new dreams and forge new connections.

She took a deep breath, resolved to create her own path forward. She would not let her loneliness define her; instead, she would use it as a catalyst for change.

Coinciding with her fortieth birthday, she sat in the coffee shop, talking to herself: "Happy birthday... Whispering it alone to myself, sitting here with the door behind me, reminiscing back in that old London coffee shop at the end of the street. Sipping my hot coffee like it's my lifeline, under the watchful gaze of the aged bay window painted in red. Countless are the times this black frame with branching cracks has listened to the sighs of lost souls who sat beside it. Even their sorrows etched wrinkles on her ribs...

Years have taught me how to succeed in this individualistic society, where achievement is paved with the currency of personal sacrifice. But one thing eludes me still - the feeling of solitude... Until a hand grabbed me and pulled me out of the café, «Are you ready for the journey, my love?" Henry murmured to her as he extended his hand, a reassuring gesture that invited me into the waiting car.

"Where are we going?" I finally asked, breaking the silence as Henry started to drive, his smile warm and reassuring in the dim glow of the dashboard lights.

"Somewhere special," he replied cryptically, his eyes twinkling with a hint of mystery.

"A place where we can make memories together." And with that, we embarked on our journey into the night, leaving behind the familiar and stepping into the unknown, hand in hand, hearts intertwined with the promise of new experiences and shared adventures.

Ten years of struggle, sacrifice; until I became who I am today—Cheetah, wife of the rabbit.

---

The immigration minister hurried down the saffron-covered corridor towards the grand meeting hall, his footsteps echoing softly against the shimmering floor adorned with diamonds and turquoise rocks that sparkled in the ambient light. Lining his path were cacti and philodendron with other tropical plants, their leaves swaying gently with each of his strides. Each plant seemed to whisper ancient secrets as he passed their presence both soothing and eerie.

Approaching the door, he was greeted by a marvelously crafted emerald shell glowing with a mesmerising emerald-green hue. The archway seemed alive, pulsating with an energy that tingled his skin as he passed through its threshold.

Inside, the atmosphere shifted palpably. The air hummed with anticipation, carrying the weight of decisions that would shape destinies.

There, upon an ancient throne carved from the timber of age-old trees, sat the king. His presence commanded the room, radiating an aura of wisdom and timeless power that seemed to emanate from the very walls themselves. As the minister approached, he could feel the gravity of the moment pressing down upon him.

"Your Majesty," his voice steady despite the nerves that churned within him, "today we announce the closure of the immigration programme to Eleanor Island for the year 2024-2025."

The king raised a hand, and the room fell into an expectant silence. His gaze, penetrating yet compassionate, swept over the assembled advisors before settling back on the minister. "And how many applications have we received?" he asked, his voice resonating with a depth that spoke of the burdens he bore.

"25 million applications, Your Majesty," replied the minister, each word carefully chosen to convey both the enormity and the urgency of the situation.

The king nodded thoughtfully, his eyes narrowing slightly as he considered the implications. With a gesture that seemed almost casual, the walls around them expanded, revealing a panoramic view of distant islands floating amidst a sea of stars. It was a breathtaking sight, one that seemed to stretch the boundaries of reality itself.

"We must now take steps to acquire nearby islands," the king declared, his words carrying the weight of inevitability. "It is our duty to provide hope and opportunity, even in the face of such overwhelming demand."

The minister felt a surge of determination mingled with apprehension. The path ahead was fraught with challenges and uncertainties, but as he looked out at the shimmering islands in the distance, he knew that they represented more than just land. They were symbols of possibility, of a future where dreams could take root and flourish.

This enchanting scene marked a pivotal moment in their shared journey, where the intersection of realism and magical realism illuminated the complexities of immigration, identity, and governance. It was a narrative woven with threads of hope and resilience, reminding them all that even in the most extraordinary circumstances, and the therians' savagery, humanity's spirit endured.

◈ The end ◈

## The Final Chapter

Here, at the end of this book, Eleanor smiled and spoke two words for the first time in sixteen years.

"Sixteen years! What did she say, sir? And what caused all this silence?"

Well, I had told you before about the river incident involving Jagger, which was merely a figment of my imagination. I don't know if I narrated it well or failed, as you know I am neither a literary writer nor a talented poet. I put in all my effort and retrieved every word from my linguistic repertoire to write these lines. But the reality of what happened that day is a tragedy by all measures. Jagger didn't know how to swim and didn't jump into the shallow waters but into the strong current leading to the concrete-built canal tunnel, which flows into the dam.

As for Eleanor, she had indeed tried to stop him, but when they found her in front of the canal wearing her mask, what could they say? It was clear they would accuse her.

"Maybe you say this because she is your daughter, or are you certain?"

Indeed, she told me everything when she returned before slipping into deep silence, especially after Jagger's father filed a lawsuit against us and accused her of madness. She stayed with us at home for ten years, but after her mother's death, I had no other option but the mental hospital. Those were tough days, but what could I do? I sometimes had to be away from home for ten days at a time for work.

"Yes, I'm sorry, I can't even imagine the situation," said the host.

"Well, what happened next?"

"I always visited her as soon as I returned from work to greet her and talk to her, hoping she might hear me. She was like a body without a soul, eating a little in silence and standing by the window a lot in silence—everything in silence. Until one day, I decided to do something for her and gifted her book that I wrote for her. I rewrote the history of her life, transforming her sorrows into joys, separation into reunion, and death into birth."

"That's a beautiful and heartfelt gesture," the host said. "What happened after you gave her the book?"

The nurse told me that on that day, as she was cleaning Eleanor, she noticed her reading the book. Seeing that only two pages remained, the nurse remarked, 'It looks like you're almost finished.' Moments later, while trimming Eleanor's nails, she heard her say, 'Thank you, Dad Thank you, Dad,' clutching the book to her chest.

"It took an entire day for Eleanor's psychiatrist to arrive and inform me of the situation. I was out of town and returned two days after he called me. Instead of going home, I went straight to the hospital to ask about her.

'Where is she?' I asked the nurse. 'She's in her room,' the nurse replied.

I entered the room and found her lying on her right side, a smile on her face as she hugged the book. I sat in front of her and called out softly, 'Eleanor, Eleanor!' Then, I began to cry when I realized she had passed away."

## ◈ The end ◈

Milton Keynes UK
Ingram Content Group UK Ltd.
UKHW031114080824
446563UK00001B/68